"What Have You Done To Me?" Luke Asked Softly.

He reached out and cupped her cheek with his hand. Her skin was soft and warm, and he lightly stroked it with his fingertips.

Her gray eyes flashed. "What are *you* doing?"

"Good question," murmured Luke. "But the only answer I can come up with is that I'm not doing enough."

Brenna licked her lips, and he followed the movement with avid eyes. "I won't hurt you, Brenna. Don't be afraid of me."

"I'm not!" she exclaimed fiercely.

"If you're not afraid, prove it, Brenna."

"By doing what?"

He gave a tug, pulling her against him. "I'll think of something."

"Have you lost your mind?" Brenna gaped at him. "I'm almost nine months pregnant!"

Dear Reader,

The year 2000 has been a special time for Silhouette, as we've celebrated our 20th anniversary. Readers from all over the world have written to tell us what they love about our books, and we'd like to share with you part of a letter from Carolyn Dann of Grand Bend, Ontario, who's a fan of Silhouette Desire. Carolyn wrote, "I like the storylines...the characters...the front covers... All the characters in the books are the kind of people you like to read about. They're all down-to-earth, everyday people." And as a grand finale to our anniversary year, Silhouette Desire offers six of your favorite authors for an especially memorable month's worth of passionate, powerful, provocative reading!

We begin the lineup with the always wonderful Barbara Boswell's MAN OF THE MONTH, *Irresistible You,* in which a single woman nine months pregnant meets her perfect hero while on jury duty. The incomparable Cait London continues her exciting miniseries FREEDOM VALLEY with *Slow Fever.* Against a beautiful Montana backdrop, the oldest Bennett sister is courted by a man who spurned her in their teenage years. And *A Season for Love,* in which Sheriff Jericho Rivers regains his lost love, continues the new miniseries MEN OF BELLE TERRE by beloved author BJ James.

Don't miss the thrilling conclusion to the Desire miniseries FORTUNE'S CHILDREN: THE GROOMS in Peggy Moreland's *Groom of Fortune.* Elizabeth Bevarly will delight you with *Monahan's Gamble.* And *Expecting the Boss's Baby* is the launch title of Leanne Banks's new miniseries, MILLION DOLLAR MEN, which offers wealthy, philanthropic bachelors guaranteed to seduce you.

We hope all readers of Silhouette Desire will treasure the gift of this special month.

Happy holidays!

Joan Marlow Golan

Joan Marlow Golan
Senior Editor, Silhouette Desire

Please address questions and book requests to:
Silhouette Reader Service
U.S.: 3010 Walden Ave., P.O. Box 1325, Buffalo, NY 14269
Canadian: P.O. Box 609, Fort Erie, Ont. L2A 5X3

Irresistible You
BARBARA BOSWELL

Silhouette® Desire®

Published by Silhouette Books
America's Publisher of Contemporary Romance

SILHOUETTE BOOKS

ISBN 0-373-76333-6

IRRESISTIBLE YOU

Visit Silhouette at www.eHarlequin.com

Printed in U.S.A.

Books by Barbara Boswell

Silhouette Desire

Rule Breaker #558
Another Whirlwind Courtship #583
The Bridal Price #609
The Baby Track #651
License To Love #685
Double Trouble #749
Triple Treat #787
The Best Revenge #821
Family Feud #877
The Engagement Party #932
The Wilde Bunch #943
Who's the Boss? #1069
The Brennan Baby #1123
That Marriageable Man! #1147
Forever Flint #1243
Bachelor Doctor #1303
Irresistible You #1333

Silhouette Books

*Fortune's Children
Stand-In Bride*

*A Fortune's Children Wedding:
The Hoodwinked Bride*

BARBARA BOSWELL

loves writing about families. "I guess family has been a big influence on my writing," she says. "I particularly enjoy writing about how my characters' family relationships affect them."

When Barbara isn't writing and reading, she's spending time with her *own* family—her husband, three daughters and three cats, whom she concedes are the true bosses of their home! She has lived in Europe, but now makes her home in Pennsylvania. She collects miniatures and holiday ornaments, tries to avoid exercise and has somehow found the time to write over twenty category romances.

IT'S OUR 20th ANNIVERSARY!
December 2000 marks the end of our anniversary year.
We hope you've enjoyed the many special titles already
offered, and we invite you to sample those wonderful titles
on sale this month! 2001 promises to be every bit as
exciting, so keep coming back to Silhouette Books,
where love comes alive....

Desire

 MAN OF THE MONTH

#1333 Irresistible You
Barbara Boswell

 Freedom Valley

#1334 Slow Fever
Cait London

MEN Belle Terre

#1335 A Season for Love
BJ James

The Grooms

#1336 Groom of Fortune
Peggy Moreland

#1337 Monahan's Gamble
Elizabeth Bevarly

 MILLION DOLLAR MEN

#1338 Expecting the Boss's Baby
Leanne Banks

Romance

 Bachelor Gulch

#1486 Sky's Pride and Joy
Sandra Steffen

#1487 Hunter's Vow
Susan Meier

 THE BRUBAKER BRIDES

#1488 Montana's Feisty Cowgirl
Carolyn Zane

 SINGLE DOCTOR DADS

#1489 Rachel and the M.D.
Donna Clayton

 STORK EXPRESS

#1490 Mixing Business...with Baby
Diana Whitney

#1491 His Special Delivery
Belinda Barnes

Special Edition

 AND BABY MAKES THREE THE NEXT GENERATION

#1363 The Delacourt Scandal
Sherryl Woods

#1364 The McCaffertys: Thorne
Lisa Jackson

#1365 The Cowboy's Gift-Wrapped Bride
Victoria Pade

Rumor Has It... **#1366 Lara's Lover**
Penny Richards

#1367 Mother in a Moment
Allison Leigh

 Here Come the Brides

#1368 Expectant Bride-To-Be
Nikki Benjamin

Intimate Moments

#1045 Special Report
Merline Lovelace/Maggie Price/
Debra Cowan

a Year of Loving Dangerously **#1046 Strangers When We Married**
Carla Cassidy

#1047 A Very...Pregnant New Year's
Doreen Roberts

#1048 Mad Dog and Annie
Virginia Kantra

#1049 Mirror, Mirror
Linda Randall Wisdom

#1050 Everything But a Husband
Karen Templeton

One

─────

Jury Duty!

Luke Minteer was still in shock. As of tomorrow morning he was supposed to be a juror in a civil case. And from the few facts the opposing lawyers had revealed about the case during the juror interview, Luke already deemed it a major time waster. Of *his* valuable time!

This, after he'd been such a good sport about the situation. Despite the major inconvenience of being summoned to join his fellow citizens in the potential jury pool, he had dutifully—albeit grudgingly—shown up at the courthouse for the selection. That should have been the end of it, as far as he was concerned.

He expected to be rejected; he was counting on it. For the first time ever, rejection was infinitely appealing, and his past days as a tarnished hotshot political operative seemed to guarantee it. Who would want the likes of *him* on a jury?

Apparently the judge and the attorneys on both sides would—because he'd been selected.

Desperately he looked around at the other chosen jurors sitting with him in the box, while a bailiff instructed them on their upcoming obligations. They were now expected to put their lives on hold, to be held captive in a courtroom— and all because two idiots, aided and abetted by their mercenary lawyers, had decided to sue each other.

He was Luke Minteer! He didn't do jury duty!

Eight of the chosen were years older than he was. *Decades* older! Two young men who appeared to be in their early twenties sported multiple tattoos and piercings on various parts of their bodies—their eyebrows, their noses, their lips and of course their ears, with at least ten earrings per lobe.

Luke glanced at the final juror, the young woman sitting next to him, who was very visibly pregnant. She looked like a teenager, though he knew she couldn't be. In the state of Pennsylvania, jury duty fell only to those who'd reached the legal age of twenty-one.

Luke couldn't gauge how advanced her pregnancy was. Unmarried and not a parent, he steered clear of the mysteries of pregnant women.

What mattered in this situation was that she was unmistakably pregnant, the young men looked like circus freaks, and the elderly people were very, very old. One of them coughed continually.

Luke groaned. "I don't have a prayer of getting out of this."

"You just said exactly what I was thinking," said the pregnant woman, looking surprised.

Luke was surprised, too. He hadn't intended to speak his own thoughts aloud like that. Another sign of how rattled he was by his unexpected inclusion.

"They must be desperate for jurors to pick this crew,"

she murmured, now voicing his observation. "I'm due to deliver my baby in six weeks. The lawyers for both sides said the trial would be all wrapped up long before then, though," she added hopefully.

"Don't believe everything you hear," Luke grumbled. "Especially when a lawyer says it. I worked in politics. I know."

"Didn't you tell them you worked in politics?" Her gray eyes widened. "It seems that would instantly disqualify you."

"Why would I be disqualified on those grounds?" Never mind he'd believed the same thing—wrongly. "This case has nothing to do with politics, it's a battle-of-the-sexes case."

"And a really stupid one," she added glumly.

"You took the words right out of my mouth." Luke heaved a groan. "The facts of this case read like the rejected proposal for a really bad book. Guy gives girl engagement ring, then dumps her. She refuses to give back the ring, which he claims is a family heirloom—and which he wants for his new fiancée. Let's call her fiancée two. So he sues fiancée one to get the ring back."

"But fiancée one claims the ring was a gift, hers to keep," his pregnant fellow juror interjected.

"Or to sell. In order to finance the breast implants she claims are essential to her career as a nude dancer," Luke added dryly.

"And she also countersues him for harassment or interfering with her civil right to work or whatever." The young woman rolled her eyes heavenward. "I tuned out at that point."

"Did you hear that both parties are demanding punitive damages for their emotional pain and suffering? As if either one feels any emotion except pure greed—and possibly revenge."

"Why can't they settle it themselves like civilized human beings? Why do they have to go to court and drag all of us into it?" she railed. "Who can side with either one, anyway? He's a fickle cheapskate and she's a manipulative—"

She paused for a moment.

"Perhaps litigious, silicone-endowed nude dancer is the term you were looking for?"

"I had something a bit less flattering in mind. Already, I can't stand either one of them, and I've never even met them."

"Did you say that to the lawyers?" quizzed Luke.

She nodded. "Oh, yes."

"So did I. Must be why we were picked. Better to dislike them both than to side with one. The lawyers would consider that fair and impartial."

"It's a lot like politics after all," she said thoughtfully. "Where you don't like either candidate but are supposed to vote for one. It boils down to the lesser of two evils at worst, or at best, two jerks."

"Evil or jerk." Luke held back a sigh. "I'm going to take a wild guess that you think all politicians are unlikable, morally corrupt, sleazy…. Feel free to jump in and stop me at any time."

She didn't. Which apparently meant she agreed with his assessment?

"I was attempting to be ironic," he said to enlighten her. "There are exceptions to the corrupt politician stereotype, you know."

"I'll take your word on that." She looked bored with the subject.

From his past work in the field, Luke was aware that politics tended either to bore or inflame, and unless one was canvassing for votes, a change of topic was advisable. Still, he was unable to let it go.

"One exception is my brother, Matt Minteer. He's a congressman." Luke's voice held a note of fraternal pride. "Matt is the representative for the Johnstown district, which includes this county, so that would make him your congressman."

"Matt Minteer," she repeated. "Is he the one who fired his own brother for dirty tricks or nasty campaign tactics or something like that? I heard about it when I moved here last year."

This time Luke didn't suppress his sigh. He let it out heavily. "Yeah, that would be Matt. The nasty, dirty-tricks-playing brother is me. I was fired two years and eight months ago, but the story is still being told, I see."

"And those lawyers picked you for the jury anyway?" The young woman was incredulous. "Wow! They are really, *really* desperate."

"No charges were ever filed against me. It's not as if I'm a convicted felon." Luke was defensive. "Although as far as my brother's staff is concerned, I might as well be. They're a very traditional group, set like cement in the old ways. When I tried to be innovative and competitive, to take some risks and implement some new ideas and methods for—"

"Translation," she cut in. "When you used dirty tricks and nasty tactics, they didn't approve, and you got the ax."

Luke scowled. "Are you always so…blunt?"

Though she'd pretty much summed up the situation, it didn't mean he liked hearing it.

"Yes," she said…bluntly.

"Well, why should you be different from everybody else?" Luke was aware that his voice held just the faintest trace of self-pity. He didn't care. "No one else in the district bothers to hold back their opinion of me, including my own family. Everybody reminds me that, though to the world at large I may be a bestselling crime fiction writer these days, in this district, I'm still Congressman Minteer's brother, the weasel.''

She arched her dark brows. "Crime fiction?"

Luke brightened. Even the locals who disapproved of him as an innovative, risk-taking political mastermind bought his book. Everybody, everywhere, had, bringing him national success as an author.

"I wrote a bestselling crime novel about a serial killer that was published in hardcover and did well and then hit number one on the *New York Times* list when it came out in paperback. It's still on the bestseller lists, although farther down by now, of course, and—"

"I don't read crime fiction, and I'd *never* read about serial killers," she said disapprovingly. "Why would anyone want to read about such evil and ugliness? Why would anyone want to write it?"

"You aren't the first to ask that question." Instead of taking offense, Luke grinned. "In fact, most of my family does. But I do have one favorite aunt who tells me to make the crimes in my next book even more grisly."

"Well, I don't agree with your favorite aunt. Glorifying crime is…is toxic."

"I don't glorify—" He began to argue, but inevitably, his sense of humor kicked in. "You are *brutally* frank. Opinionated, too. Those lawyers in this trial might think you're a malleable little mommy, but it looks like the joke is on them. You'll probably hang the jury and they'll have to try the case all over again."

The bailiff appeared again, instructing the chosen twelve to report back to the courtroom tomorrow morning at nine-thirty for the beginning of the trial. Then he excused them for the day.

Everybody stood up. None of the selected jurors looked happy with their fate.

"It's four o'clock," muttered one of the older men.

"The day is already completely wasted. Why did they take so darn long to pick us? All those foolish questions they asked us..."

"I had to take two buses to get here," complained an elderly woman. "Now I have to take two to get home— *and* do it for heaven only knows how many more days, until this is all over."

"I'm bringing my knitting with me every day," said another woman defiantly. "I have to finish an afghan for my great-niece's new baby in time for Christmas. That's little more than a month away."

The two pierced, tattooed young men slunk off. Luke stared after them, bemused. He noticed that the pregnant woman was looking at them, too.

"What are the odds of two jurors sporting identical dragon tattoos that stretch the length of their arms?" he murmured. "I'd never put that in a book. My editor would say, 'Come on, Luke, that's too over the top.'"

"Sometimes truth is stranger than fiction. Which is a creepy thought, considering some of the fiction being written these days."

"I assume that's another potshot at my writing career?" drawled Luke. "Nobody can accuse you of being subtle."

She and Luke faced each other.

"Since we're fellow jurors, we might as well introduce ourselves. I'm Luke Minteer." He offered his hand to her.

"Brenna Morgan." She shook his hand but withdrew her own quickly.

"You look like you want to wipe your palm on something. Don't worry, I'm not infectious," Luke said drolly. "I'm merely the bad-guy brother of your good and honorable congressman, and that is not contagious."

She looked ready to debate the point. "You switched to a career writing crime novels about serial killers."

"And you don't know which is worse. My political chi-

canery was disgusting, but my writing is morbid and sick.''
He smiled slightly at her startled look. ''No, I'm not a mind
reader, Mrs. Morgan. I'm just quoting my mom and my
sisters, my grandmother and my aunts, except for Helen.
You'd get along famously with them. They never miss a
chance to lecture me on the perils of writing about evil.''

''But you enjoy writing about evil?''

She was looking at him as if he were Satan incarnate on
a book tour. Luke felt compelled to offer some sort of defense.

''Look, I'll try to explain to you the way I've tried to
explain it to the family. Inventing a crime and a case and
solving it is fascinating. You can enter the mind of your
characters and set up the cat-and-mouse game between the
criminal and the police. Plus, on the practical side, it's been
a very good career move.''

Okay, he wanted to brag a little about his writing success, Luke acknowledged to himself. Was that so bad, in
light of the fact he'd been viewed as a disgrace to the Minteer clan, as the district pariah? His writing had elevated
him to something akin to celebrity status.

Celebrity or pariah? That choice was a no-brainer.

''A person's got to make a living, you know,'' he added,
with a practiced touch of boyish charm.

Brenna Morgan stared impassively at him, uncharmed.
''And since you'd already been kicked out of dirty-tricks
politics, creating serial killers was the logical next step?
There's nothing in between? Not anything in the retail industry or in the business world or the—''

''Aha! Now you're joking. I see the glint of humor in
your eyes, despite your best efforts to hide it behind that
deadpan facade.''

This time Luke flashed his most winning smile, the one
on the back cover of his book's dust jacket. He'd gotten

fan mail based on that picture, from women who hadn't bothered to read the book.

Brenna slowly, almost reluctantly smiled back.

Luke knew she would. No woman was immune to his special smile, not even pregnant ones who thoroughly disapproved of him and his profession. That is, unless she happened to be related to him. To his female relatives, his smile and his charm were distinctly underwhelming.

"I really wasn't joking," Brenna insisted.

"Sure you were. Those big gray eyes of yours are still shining with amusement."

"No, they aren't."

"Are you one of those types who always has to have the last word? Your poor husband—and those hapless lawyers who have no idea that they've chosen an intractable force of nature to be on their jury." Luke laughed. "Yeah, it'll be a hung jury, all right."

The two of them started walking toward the door, toward freedom. They fell into step, side-by-side. Luke cast a swift glance over at her.

He always noted a woman's height, and he made no exception this time. She was wearing flat shoes, which allowed him to correctly estimate that Brenna Morgan was not quite five-four. At five feet ten inches, he seemed to be towering over her. Luke enjoyed the sensation in spite of himself.

After all, he'd made peace with his less-than-six-foot height *years* ago. He didn't mind being the shortest of the four Minteer brothers, he didn't care that his three sisters were nearly his height. That two of his teen nephews already were as tall as he was and were still growing.

It wouldn't be long until he was surpassed in height by another generation of Minteer brothers. Not that Luke minded, of course.

And to prove it to himself and everybody else in the

world, he deliberately dated tall women, women close to his own height or even taller, especially in very high heels. He liked the elegance, the challenge of height. He was *completely* comfortable being one of the less-tall Minteers and didn't need short women to make him feel—well, six-feet tall.

In fact, he assiduously avoided pairing up with a petite woman. To prove his point to himself and everybody else.

He cast another surreptitious glance at Brenna Morgan.

She was pretty. That renegade thought fleetingly crossed Luke's mind, surprising him. He did not, as a rule, take note of a pregnant woman's looks. A pregnant woman obviously belonged to another guy, and he wasn't the type who poached on his brother man's territory.

He might be viewed as a snake by some—okay, by many—but he did have a certain code of ethics that he followed. Cheating with another man's woman was strictly taboo.

Besides, a pregnant woman was a mother-to-be, and mothers deserved the utmost respect. The Minteer brothers had that canon drilled into them by their own mother and grandmothers, by their aunts and great-aunts and older cousins, too.

He certainly respected mothers too much to think of them as pretty, Luke reminded himself. Because thoughts of prettiness too easily led to thoughts of desirability, which logically progressed to thoughts of sex.

Mothers, those paragons of maternal virtue, were not sexy! At least, they weren't to Luke Minteer.

But Brenna Morgan, with her long black hair curving just over her shoulders, her thick bangs accentuating high cheekbones and big, clear gray eyes fringed with dark lashes, with her firm little chin and full, sensual lips… No, not sensual, he quickly amended. Sensual and pregnant just didn't go together.

Still, Brenna Morgan was definitely a pretty woman.

To cleanse himself of the disturbing thought, Luke allowed his gaze to drift over her totally nonexistent figure. She looked like a balloon overinflated with helium, the skirt of her blue maternity dress swirling around her swollen feet and ankles.

Luke expelled what might have been a sigh of relief. He admired long, shapely legs on a woman. Though he couldn't see Brenna's legs under the long blue skirt, her puffy ankles certainly failed his desirability test.

As well they should. She was pregnant, some kid's mother-to-be.

She was some guy's wife. She was of no interest to him whatsoever.

"Is your husband going to be ticked off that you're stuck with jury duty and that your poor unborn child is going to be exposed to lawyers and their sleazy clients for days on end?" Luke asked jovially, purposefully, as they reached the main entrance of the building.

Brenna, in the midst of pulling on her oversize light-brown parka, looked up at him, in that serious, earnest way of hers. "I don't have a husband. This baby is mine and mine alone."

She pushed the double doors open and walked off, leaving him staring after her, his jaw agape.

"You were picked for jury duty in your condition? Are they nuts? Did you tell them the baby is due in six weeks?" Cassie Walsh, Brenna's next-door neighbor, was outraged on her behalf.

Cassie's three-year-old daughter, Abigail, sat on the floor, transfixed by a video of *Winnie the Pooh,* and didn't look up as Cassie rolled an ottoman toward Brenna, who was resting in the armchair.

"I told them." Brenna wearily propped her swollen feet

up on the ottoman. "It didn't matter. The judge told us at the beginning of the day that they were cracking down on people getting out of jury duty."

"How can you be expected to sit for hours when you're so far along in your pregnancy?" Cassie demanded. "Can't you get an excuse from your doctor?"

"But then my name would go back in the jury pool and I might be chosen after I have the baby. I'd rather get it over with now. Anyway, sitting in the courtroom isn't any different from sitting in an office all day—or me sitting in my studio drawing for hours, right?"

"I suppose so."

"Uh, one of the jurors is the brother of our congressman, Matt Minteer," Brenna added, keeping her voice carefully casual.

It bothered her that she had to make an *effort* to sound uninterested. She should be naturally uninterested! Even worse was the realization of how much she wanted to talk about Luke Minteer to Cassie, because she knew that Cassie's brother, Steve, was a lobbyist in Harrisburg and a reliable source of information about Pennsylvania politicians. And maybe about the brothers of politicians, too?

Brenna blushed. She was attempting to pump her friend for information about a guy—like some infatuated thirteen-year-old! A wave of hot embarrassment swamped her.

"Which brother?" asked Cassie. "Matthew Minteer has three brothers, Mark, Luke and John."

"Luke," mumbled Brenna. She still couldn't believe she was playing this game. It was so very unlike her!

"Ah, Cambria County's most notorious bachelor." Cassie chuckled. "He'll sure bring a wealth of experience to any jury!"

Brenna stared silently into space. She was too preoccupied with Luke Minteer, and that was not a good thing, she warned herself. She could visualize him so clearly in her

mind's eye, it was as if he were standing right in the room
with her....

Brenna gulped. Luke Minteer was one of those too-
handsome, too-charismatic, too-masculine-for-his-own-
good men. Certainly, for *her* own good.

She saw his thick, dark hair, cut slightly long, which
gave him a certain rakish air. And then there were those
blue eyes, such a brilliant and distinct shade of blue. The
strong line of his jaw, his well-shaped mouth. Oh, that
mouth!

Brenna laid her palms against her flushed cheeks to cool
them. But those visuals of Luke Minteer in the courtroom
kept coming.

His long-sleeved blue chambray shirt seemed to accen-
tuate, not conceal, the breadth of his shoulders and chest
and the rippling muscles in his arms. And he'd boldly worn
jeans, in spite of the dress code printed on the jury sum-
mons that said "no jeans or shorts allowed."

Never mind that half the people who'd shown up were
wearing jeans, too, Luke Minteer wore his jeans too well,
like a sexy cowboy in a magazine ad. Brenna gave her head
a quick shake to dislodge *that* uncensored thought.

By wearing jeans Luke Minteer had deliberately flaunted
the rules, that's what she intended to think. And what else
could you expect from a political dirty trickster who'd been
fired by his own brother? Brenna tried hard to summon up
some hearty disdain for the man.

Instead, she found herself picturing his hands.

They were large and strong, with long, well-shaped fingers and short, clean nails. That she had been aware of such
minute details, had seemingly committed them to memory,
appalled her. And then additional mental pictures flashed
before her, scenes that dropped below his chest to his flat
stomach and—

Brenna sat bolt upright in the chair.

"Brenna, are you all right?" Cassie was immediately concerned.

Brenna nodded weakly. "A…little twinge. A cramp, I think."

"That'll keep happening the farther along you get," Cassie, a mother of three, said sympathetically. "Braxton-Hicks contractions. Try not to let it worry you."

Brenna gulped. She wasn't worried about twinges and cramps; she'd read all about them, she even expected them. But this alarming awareness of Luke Minteer…

That was totally unexpected. What was the matter with her? Was she losing her mind? She was heading into her ninth month of pregnancy, and the last thing she should be thinking about was—

And suddenly a blanket of calm descended over her. Of course. She was heading into her ninth month of pregnancy…. That explained it all.

Hormones!

Every pregnancy book she'd read—and there were plenty—had claimed that her hormones would go into overdrive and could cause wildly irrational thinking, emotions and even behavior. So far she had remained remarkably immune from all that, but now it appeared she had succumbed at last.

"You had a long, tiring day, Brenna," Cassie continued, her tone soothing. "Why don't you stay for dinner tonight? Ray has a meeting at the high school and will be home late, and Brandon and Tim are eating at their friend Josh's house. I made macaroni and cheese for Abigail and me, and there's plenty of it. *And* we have chocolate cake for dessert, my grandma's recipe."

"Thanks, Cassie, but I…I really should go home," Brenna said weakly. "I ought to work on my—"

"Stay!" Cassie insisted. "I'll fill you in on your fellow juror, Luke Minteer. According to my brother, Steve, Luke was kind of a legend around Harrisburg when Matt was in state government there, but he managed to contain himself back then.''

"What kind of legend?'' murmured Brenna, in spite of herself.

Her unborn baby kicked so hard, the movements caused the material of her blue dress to bob and weave.

"Oh, the kind who played mind games to psych out opponents—and who played lots of games with lots of different women, if you know what I mean.'' Cassie cast a quick glance toward little Abigail, but the child was engrossed in the video and paying no attention to the adult conversation.

"Luke was a player, and I'm sorry to say that in those bad old days, my brother used to be one, too,'' Cassie said, lowering her voice a bit. "Steve and Luke moved in the same circles. But at least Steve matured and reformed and is a good family man now,'' she added, clearly relieved by the transformation.

"Not Luke Minteer, though,'' guessed Brenna.

Not that she cared, she assured herself. She was simply passing the time, chatting with Cassie until dinnertime. She'd decided to stay; the macaroni and cheese and chocolate cake were too tempting to pass up. She could work later this evening.

"No, not Luke,'' Cassie agreed. "Matt Minteer was elected to Congress and Luke went along to D.C. as his administrative aide, the same position he'd had in Harrisburg. But in D.C., Luke was unleashed. He ran wild down there.''

"How?'' Brenna prompted. "Uh, not that I want a detailed account,'' she added hastily, her face flushing again.

"I'll give you the abridged version. Luke got in with a very fast social crowd plus a very nasty political crowd. Maybe he could've stayed unnoticed in one, but not both.

Steve said rumors about him were constantly flying from D.C. to Harrisburg <u>and, of course,</u> back here to the district. Matt ended up firing Luke. Boy, were the Minteers mad!''

"At Luke or at Matt for firing his brother—or both?''

"At Luke, only at Luke. They let it be known how much they disapproved of him and encouraged everybody else to tell Luke their own unfavorable opinions of him, too.''

"I wonder why he came back here?'' Brenna mused. "It seems like a strange choice for someone like him, to come back to a small town and be ostracized and criticized by his own family.''

"Maybe he was trying to get back on their good side. But if he was, it didn't work. And then he wrote this really successful novel. I heard it's going to be made into a movie, which would mean even more money, but his family still disapproves of him.'' Cassie shrugged. "They're a tough crowd, the Minteers.''

"He has a favorite aunt who likes his book. He, um, mentioned her.''

"I don't know which one she is. There are so many Minteers in the area, especially when you count the aunts, uncles and cousins. Abigail goes to preschool with Luke's brother John's little boy, David. Sounds like some sort of six-degrees-of-separation chain, doesn't it?'' Cassie smiled. "Or maybe fate?''

Brenna swallowed hard. "What do you mean?''

"Well, who knows what could happen between you and Luke when—''

"Nothing,'' Brenna said firmly. "Cassie, I'm having a baby, for heaven's sakes.''

"Who needs a father. Because there isn't one in the picture.''

"And from what you've told me, Luke Minteer sounds just like the kind of man who would love to step in and play daddy to someone else's child.'' Brenna's voice dripped sarcasm. "As if he would ever find a pregnant woman attractive in the first place!"

"Okay, I concede your point." Cassie gave up. "The only thing that will happen involving you and Luke Minteer and jury duty is a verdict."

Brenna ran her hand through her hair. "And maybe not even that. What if it's a hung jury?"

She thought of Luke's amused prediction that she would be the one to hang the jury, but didn't share the remark with Cassie. She didn't want her friend to know how long she and Luke had talked, especially after Cassie's outlandish speculations.

Besides, she'd already spent too much time thinking about Luke Minteer—and way too much time talking about him to Cassie. It was puzzling, and disturbing, too.

And then there was the most puzzling, disturbing thing of all—that remark she'd made to him upon leaving the courthouse.

Why hadn't she simply played along with Luke Minteer's belief that she was married? Why hadn't she pretended that a "Mr. Morgan" actually existed?

Luke had assumed one did, that she was a married woman—until she'd quashed that notion flat.

Why had she done it? Brenna mused throughout the evening. By morning she still didn't have the answer.

Two

All twelve jurors arrived on time the next morning for the beginning of the trial. They introduced themselves to each other, and one of the older men, Roger Hollister, was elected foreman. The lawyers for both sides seemed pleased with the jurors' first group decision; Hollister, whose nickname was Sarge, had served in World War II and knew a thing or two about leadership.

In the jury box before the opening argument, Luke once again sat next to Brenna Morgan. A natural gravitation process had already occurred among the twelve. Sarge Hollister and the other two men in his age group sat together, as did the five elderly women. The two pierced and tattooed young men, both named Jason with different surnames, stuck together, which left Brenna and Luke with nobody but each other.

Or so Luke told himself. Never mind that in his political incarnation, he had prided himself in fitting in with any group, regardless of age or sex. That was then, this was now, and he and Brenna were their own group strictly by default.

He glanced over at her. She'd gone for comfort over formality today, trading in yesterday's blue maternity dress for black slacks and a long bottle-green top. He had opted for jeans again—after reading the prissy advisory not to wear them to court, of course he would never wear anything else—and an equally casual plaid flannel shirt.

But Brenna had followed the dress code, such as it was. She'd pulled her dark hair high in a ponytail, and the ends of it brushed against the nape of her neck. Luke's eyes lingered on the soft, creamy-white skin exposed there, and he quickly lowered his gaze.

She looked as if she had a beachball stuffed under her shirt. Her breasts and belly seemed to merge into one big shapeless bulge, but her black tapered pants revealed that despite her advanced pregnancy, her legs were nicely shaped. Her ankles weren't swollen today. He noticed that, too.

Luke frowned.

"Why aren't you married?" he blurted out in a low whisper.

Brenna turned to look at him, visibly startled by the question. Luke himself was startled. He was doing it again—blabbing his thoughts aloud. The influence of the courthouse, perhaps? It was an old gothic-style place, vaguely creepy, where strange things might be expected to happen—like him imagining that he was being influenced by the atmosphere!

"Because I'm not," she replied coolly.

She might as well have come right out and flatly said, It's none of your business, because her answer, her voice and entire demeanor conveyed just that sentiment.

Still Luke didn't back off. "Did your boyfriend dump you when he found out you were pregnant?"

"Are you speaking from personal experience? Is that what *you* would do in a similar situation?" Brenna went on the offense, her chin rising defiantly. "Or maybe you've already done it, for all I know." She didn't meet his eyes.

"No! I didn't—I wouldn't—I've never—" Luke paused when the attorney for Brad, the plaintiff, stood and began to present his opening argument.

Brad sat at the table, listening to his side being presented, nodding his head at every point. His former fiancée, Amber, visibly bristled, grimaced and vehemently shook her head in disagreement.

Everybody in the jury box stared at the feuding former lovers—everybody except Luke Minteer, whose eyes remained riveted on Brenna.

He leaned a little closer to her, his voice low in her ear. "Don't try to turn this around and sling mud at me, lady. This isn't about *me*."

"True. It has nothing to do with you," she murmured between clenched teeth. "And please stop talking. The judge is giving us a dirty look."

"And God forbid we get on the wrong side of His Honor," taunted Luke. "We might get thrown off the jury. Wow, *that* would be a heavy price to pay."

"Excuse me." The judge pounded his gavel, interrupting the attorney. "Jurors nine and ten, conversation will be conducted outside the courtroom, not during the trial. I don't want to have to mention this again." He glowered at Brenna and Luke.

Brenna blushed and she stared at the floor. Luke shrugged, scowling, but unintimidated by the reprimand.

"Don't look so guilty," he whispered to Brenna a moment later. "It's not like we're criminals on trial here.

We're the ones giving up our time to do our civic duty so that *Brad and Amber* can stick it to each—"

"Will you please shut up!" Brenna said desperately. "We're going to get jailed for contempt of court or something if you keep—"

"Juror nine!" thundered the judge, glaring at Brenna.

She slumped lower in her chair. "I'm sorry, Your Honor."

"She isn't feeling well, Your Honor," Luke spoke up. "She is very advanced in her pregnancy and needs to take a break right now. If you would be kind enough to excuse her for a few minutes..." He stared at the judge expectantly.

The judge looked nonplussed. "I...see. All right, we'll all take a ten-minute break. Court resumes in ten minutes." He strode from the courtroom.

"If we take ten-minute breaks every ten minutes, this trial will never end," one attorney complained to the other, loud enough to be heard in the jury box.

"You guys are the ones who picked a very pregnant woman to be on your jury," Luke called back to them. "So live with it, boys."

"I'm going to the rest room," Brenna murmured, and quickly left the courtroom.

Luke was in the corridor standing against the wall when she emerged from the bathroom. She would have walked past him, but he approached her.

"I came to your rescue," he said proudly. "Pretty fast thinking on my part, hmm?"

"Is that how you see yourself? A kind of gallant knight in shining armor?" Brenna headed directly to the courtroom, Luke at her side. "What you seem to forget is that you're the reason I got in trouble in the first place."

"Honey, you got in trouble long before I came on the scene."

"If that's an attempt at wit," Brenna ground out, "it failed."

"Mmm-hmm. So you were dumped by the daddy when you told him you were pregnant?" Luke surmised with a knowing nod. "You wouldn't be so defensive and angry unless I'd really hit a nerve."

"I'm not defensive but, yes, I'm angry. Because you're a...a—"

"Jerk," Luke supplied amiably. "Weasel. Snake. Rat. I've been called all those things and much worse. Deservedly, too, no doubt. But I never knocked up a woman and walked away, leaving her, uh, holding the baby. Literally. I don't blame you for being furious, and if it helps to direct your rage at me, go ahead. Your boyfriend is lower than fungus slime and—"

"I don't have any rage to direct at you or anyone else!" Brenna exclaimed, exasperated. "I don't have a boyfriend who dumped me when he found out about the baby, either. There is no boyfriend and never was. Period."

Luke said nothing. They walked to their seats and sat down. They were the first two jurors to return to the box.

"Go on, ask me," Brenna growled, after a few more moments of Luke's silence. Oddly enough, it disturbed her more than his questions and speculations. "I can almost hear what you're thinking. So just say it."

"I'm not one to criticize anyone else for being impulsive." His lips quirked into a wry smile. "I used to call it being spontaneous back when I was your age."

"Back when you were my age?" Brenna scoffed. "That wasn't so long ago, was it? It's not like you were in World War II with Sarge and company."

"I'm thirty-five and it's been a long time since I was—" Luke gazed down at her. "Twenty-one?" he guessed. "And crossing the line from spontaneous to indiscriminate can result in—"

"I'm twenty-six. And having my baby wasn't an impulsive act, it—" She broke off and stared at him, aghast. "You think that I had multiple *spontaneous* one-night stands and wasn't careful?"

"You said you could hear what I was thinking," he reminded her.

"I didn't think it was *that!*" Her voice rose in indignation. "Ick! Sleeping around indiscriminately? *You* might have, but I would never do that."

"Don't get too self-righteous, honey. You're pregnant, and that means at least one sexual encounter with at least one man. Since you were so adamant about not having a boyfriend, naturally, I assumed you'd, er, scored with more than one guy and didn't know which one was the father of your baby. Not that I'm condemning you for that," he added. "I'm very open-minded."

"How generous of you!"

"I guess I might've sounded a bit self-righteous myself there." Chagrined, Luke took a deep breath. "I apologize."

"Don't bother, because it doesn't apply. Just because you *scored* with a string of one-night stands doesn't mean that I did. And I *do* know who the father of my baby is. I personally selected him. He's a medical student, tall, blue-eyed and blond, of Swedish-English ancestry, with no inherited diseases in his family. He has a strong bent toward the sciences but also enjoys music and sports, particularly—"

"You sound like you're reading a description out of a catalog." Luke's dark-blue eyes widened suddenly. "Good Lord, that's what you did, isn't it? That's how you picked this guy, from a…a sperm bank catalog?"

She didn't deny it. She nodded her head, confirming it.

Luke gaped at her, stunned.

"I was anything but impulsive about this." Her gray

eyes were as calm and serious as her tone. "I methodically researched everything very carefully and—"

"That's…that's so premeditated, so calculating," Luke cut in. He almost had to gasp for breath. "No, *demented* is what it is."

"You're the one who's demented! You wouldn't condemn me for a series of one-night stands or for not knowing who the father of my child is, but you're scandalized that I went to a sperm bank to—"

"Shhh!" he hushed her. "Unless you want to broadcast this to our fellow jurors, I suggest you keep quiet."

Brenna looked up to see the eight older jurors filing into the box. "You're right. I wouldn't want to shock anybody else," she murmured caustically.

"I'm not shocked, I'm just…" Luke's voice trailed off.

What exactly was he, then? He didn't know, couldn't identify the weird feelings roiling within him.

"Shocked," Brenna insisted. "And you don't like the sensation because shocking people is *your* specialty, right? You want to be the one to shock people, not the other way around."

"All right, guilty as charged. Now, can I ask you a personal question?"

She sighed. "You're going to ask it anyway, aren't you?"

"Are you gay? Is that the reason you've gone the, er, test-tube route? Because your, uh, significant other is a…a woman?"

"You should hear yourself, stammering like a shocked and disapproving candidate who is trying extra hard not to be politically incorrect." Brenna grinned. "Were you this tactful when you worked in politics?"

"Of course not—which is why I no longer work in politics. Well, are you?"

"No, I'm not gay. I don't have a significant other of

either sex, and I don't want one. There's just me and my baby, and that's all either of us will ever need.''

The two Jasons came shuffling in and had to climb over everybody to get to their seats at the end of the box. Both wore short-sleeved T-shirts, providing a clear view of the long and colorful identical dragon tattoos on their respective arms.

The sight was enough to break anyone's train of thought. Brenna and Luke stared in silence at the two dragons, then at each other. Seconds later the lawyers trooped into the courtroom with their clients. A moment after that, the judge reentered.

"Proceed, Counsel," the judge ordered.

Brad's attorney continued to explain how his client had been wronged by the duplicitous, avaricious Amber.

Luke gripped the arms of his chair.

Just me and my baby, that's all either of us will ever need. Brenna's statement swirled in his head. She sounded so sure, yet he knew she was wrong.

He had three brothers and three sisters, along with a myriad of cousins; all were married with children. He'd seen firsthand that a new mother and a newborn baby needed a lot more than each other. They needed a support system.

At the very least they needed *one* other committed person involved—first, with the pregnancy, and then with the infant itself. The baby's father ought to own that role. Every child deserved a good father.

Brad's attorney sat down, and Amber's counsel, a young woman who looked to be right out of law school, rose to her feet with an impassioned declaration about women's rights and jealous-male greed.

Luke wasn't listening. He was too astounded by his own unexpected thoughts on parenthood. It sounded as if they'd been lifted directly from one of his brother's family-values speeches.

He knew Matt believed all that stuff, but Luke didn't. At least, he thought he didn't. He'd always considered himself to be an anything-goes kind of guy.

But the thought of Brenna Morgan and her baby, alone except for each other, struck something deep within him, summoning beliefs and feelings he hadn't been aware of harboring.

Luke looked up at the high ceiling, at the old-fashioned windows that looked as though they hadn't been opened in the past century. This courthouse really was a strange place, where his brother's speeches played inside his head. Where he couldn't stop thinking about a pretty, young pregnant woman whom he didn't even know.

Except it felt as if he knew her well. From the moment they'd started talking yesterday, something had clicked, as if they'd known each other for a long, long time. As if there had never been a time when they hadn't known each other. They were open and frank and honest with each other; conversation between them came too easily for them to be total strangers.

But they'd never met...not in this lifetime.

Luke was unnerved. Now he seemed to be channeling his youngest sister, who believed in all that past-life non-sense. Luke didn't. He was a live-for-today kind of guy who tried not to think of next year, let alone a next lifetime. Or a past one...with Brenna Morgan?

A diversion was definitely in order before he lost his mind completely. Luke tried to redirect his thoughts to his new book, which was coming along fantastically well.

His newest serial killer, a charming land developer, was on the trail for fresh victims, and a small town hosting a national pageant for teenage beauty queens had invited him there, in hopes of becoming the site of his next lucrative mall....

Luke shifted in his chair, picturing the calculating killer

and the teen beauties, especially the one about to meet her doom....

And his mind abruptly went blank.

If he leaned to the right, he nearly choked on the heavy scent of musk oil emanating from one of the dragon twins. But if he leaned to the left, his shoulders brushed Brenna's and he inhaled the light, fresh scent of soap and shampoo and powder, a wholesome yet somehow alluring scent.

Luke sat straight up, suddenly, wildly alarmed. It couldn't be happening. His body was acting as if he was aroused.

He was aroused!

His pulses thundered in his head, drowning out the lawyers' voices, the whir from the heating vent in the wall, the dried fallen leaves being blown against the glass windowpanes by the wind. Brenna Morgan, sitting next to him and oblivious of the effect she was having on him, completely commanded his senses.

He could see her and smell her, but that wasn't enough. He needed more. He was filled with a faint sense of anger at his involuntary response. *This would not do!*

But he could barely stop himself from reaching over to touch her, right here in the middle of the courtroom. He desperately wanted to feel if her hair was as silky as it looked, to run his fingers along the lines of her beautifully shaped mouth. To insert his thumb inside.

Luke pictured her lips parting, then allowed his imagination free rein, erotically expanding the scene in every way....

He bent forward, straining and aching and pulsing with need.

Jason M. in the chair beside him suddenly elbowed him.

"She's hot, huh?" the younger man whispered.

Startled, Luke followed his gaze and realized that not only had Jason noticed his predicament, he had attributed it to the defendant, Amber, seated at the nearby table, her enormous chest thrust forward, her cherry-red lips pouting. Amber repeatedly flashed provocative glances at the jury, zeroing in on the three younger males in particular.

"I think she likes us," the other Jason chimed in with a snort and a chortle.

Which drew the attention of the judge. "No talking in the jury box!" he snapped.

The Jasons lapsed into sullen silence, but Luke was grateful for the reprieve.

With a sidelong gaze, Luke resumed his covert study of Brenna. Her skin, glowing and natural, her delicate features, put Amber's heavily made-up mask in the shade. As for figures…

The two Jasons might be slavering over Amber's ample assets, but Luke found himself thoroughly fascinated by the sudden visible movements of Brenna's pregnant belly. Beneath her knit shirt, the outline of the baby's head—or its rump?—was discernible as it rolled over within her.

Brenna laid her hand over her belly, as if to soothe the restless baby. And Luke, unable to stop himself, did the same thing. He felt the warmth of her belly and the movements of the unborn child beneath his fingers.

And then his hand touched Brenna's.

It was as if an electric current had passed between them.

Brenna's head jerked up, and she drew in a sharp, shocked breath. Her eyes met Luke's, and he instantly lifted his hand, unable to come up with an excuse—or at least one he considered acceptable. Not to mention believable.

"Uh, sorry," he muttered. "Irresistible impulse."

He'd tossed around that phrase in his books, not really believing such a thing existed. It was merely an easy motive to attribute to a character's behavior, almost a cliché.

Now he knew that irresistible impulses were real indeed, because he had been seized by one himself when he'd put his hand on Brenna. But how could he ever expect her to understand that, when he didn't understand it himself?

Luke watched Brenna draw back, trying to move as far from him as possible within the confines of her chair. He couldn't blame her. After all, he had invaded her personal space and touched her like some sort of out-of-control psycho.

He wrote about those—he wasn't supposed to act like one!

Luke closed his eyes and massaged his temples with his fingertips. What was happening to him? And *why?*

The morning session was adjourned for a one-hour lunch break. The two Jasons were the first to go, barreling past the other jurors and the attorneys and casting smirks at Amber as they passed her.

The eight senior members of the jury decided to go together to Peglady's, a restaurant near the courthouse. They were halfway to the door when Sarge, the foreman, turned around to look at Brenna and Luke, still standing side-by-side in the box.

"Hey, you two want to come with us?" called Sarge.

"No, thanks," Luke answered for both himself and Brenna. "Uh, you didn't want to go with them, did you?" he tacked on as the eight jurors departed with surprising speed.

"Too bad for me if I did," said Brenna. "I'd have to run to catch up with them, and I'm not in running condition these days."

"Yeah, they are hotfooting it out of here," observed Luke, unrepentant. "I guess they're hungry. Well, Peglady's serves big portions so there's plenty to eat, plus extra to take home. Too bad the food is inedible."

"How can that be? I heard one of the women, Wanda,

I think, tell the others that Peglady's is an institution here in Ebensburg.''

''Yeah, it's an institution, all right. Like prisons, schools, state hospitals. Name one of those renowned for its great cuisine.''

''Point taken.'' Brenna made her way out of the box.

Luke followed. He wasn't following her per se, he assured himself. To get out of the courtroom, he had no choice but to trail her, unless he wanted to be rude and push past her. And he did not want to be rude.

''So where are you going for lunch?'' Luke didn't like trailing behind, so he caught up to her, easily matching his long strides to her waddling ones.

It was true, she did waddle like a duck, an observation noted by his writer's eye for detail. Being so very pregnant, he knew she couldn't help it. How did she walk when she wasn't pregnant? Sexily, with her hips swaying seductively from side to side? Gracefully, like a dancer? Or—

''Maybe I'll brave Peglady's, despite the inedible food.'' Her voice intruded on his ruminations. ''At least it's close. I don't want to walk too far in the cold. What about you?''

''I think I'll go home. I live about twenty minutes outside of town, up the mountain.''

''Twenty minutes up and twenty minutes back. That won't give you much time to eat,'' Brenna pointed out.

''Approximately twenty minutes. It's sweet of you to care.''

Brenna looked up at him. His grin and the glint in his eyes matched his teasing tone.

''Don't waste your boyish-delight act on me,'' she said tartly. ''It'll probably go over well with Amber, though. She couldn't take her eyes off you and the Jasons, but I think she'd choose you, given any encouragement at all.''

''Boyish delight?'' Luke arched his brows. ''Ouch. As for Amber... Since we jurors are forbidden to discuss anything about this case among ourselves, I suppose I can't accuse you of having a jealous fit of pique because Amber was looking me over. It could be grounds for a mistrial.''

They walked into the jurors' lounge where the coatroom was located and found their coats. She had her big pale-brown parka, he had a navy-blue winter jacket that deepened the color of his eyes. Both carried their coats instead of putting them on.

Luke held the elevator doors open with his arm until she was safely inside the car. And then a group of people appeared, seemingly from nowhere, and pushed inside, shoving Brenna hard against Luke.

''Hey, people, quit rushing like a herd of stampeding buffalo,'' Luke ordered sharply. ''This woman is practically nine-months pregnant, and she was almost knocked down. Every one of you owes her an apology, and if she doesn't get one, *I'm* getting your names. And this is a courthouse, so just use your imagination as to what I'll do next.''

''Luke!'' whispered Brenna, dismayed.

Everybody in the crowded elevator began offering her abject apologies, making sure that Luke saw and heard them. She stood pressed against him, her back molded to his chest and the cradle of his thighs. His hands rested on her shoulders. They felt heavy and warm, just like his body felt against hers. She had to fight to keep from relaxing against him and melting into him. It seemed like the most natural thing in the world to do.

Heat permeated through her, and it felt good, keeping her warm even when the doors opened to a blast of the chilly November air that filled the first floor of the courthouse. The drafty entrance foyer, the source of the unwelcome cold, was just ahead of them.

''Every single one of those people told you they were sorry,'' Luke said, sounding awestruck. ''And I think they genuinely were sorry, too. Sometimes people surprise me.''

"The unanimous apologies aren't surprising at all. Everybody in that elevator knew you were watching them. They probably considered you dangerously prone to filing lawsuits. If you had told them to sing Christmas carols to me, they would've launched into a chorus of 'Joy to the World.'"

"You have a tendency to overanalyze. I suggest that you simply accept things at face value, Brenna."

"I suggest you stop making suggestions, Luke."

"That's the first time you've said my name," he murmured, staring down at her.

"So what?" Brenna didn't look at him; she kept her gaze focused well over his shoulder. "It was the first time you'd said my name, too," she added defensively.

"So you called me Luke in retaliation for me calling you Brenna?" The glint was back in his eye, the drollery in his tone. "You really go for the jugular, don't you, babe?"

She made no reply.

"I do have another suggestion to make," Luke instantly filled the silence between them. "I suggest you thank me for defending you against those boors in the elevator. I stood up for you, remember?"

"I didn't ask you to. I didn't want you to. I don't like to make a scene, and you certainly turned that elevator ride into one."

"Well, for one who doesn't like to stand out, you sure picked a helluva way to get pregnant, honey. Taking the sperm-bank route inspires curiosity, which means lots more attention than simple, old-fashioned procreation ever would've."

They stood a few feet away from the doors while they donned their coats. Luke easily shrugged into his, then helped Brenna, who was struggling with hers while also shifting her purse from side to side.

He let his hands linger on her shoulders while she fumbled with the zipper.

"I've never told anybody about—about how I got pregnant," she said, so quietly he had to strain to hear her. "And I'd appreciate it if you would keep it to yourself."

Brenna gave up on the zipper and hurried to the double doors. Luke was right behind her, and this time he pushed them open, holding them for her.

"You haven't told anybody else?" He was incredulous. "Nobody knows the truth but me?"

"No. It's a fact, I really don't like making a scene or being the center of attention. And as you pointed out, something kind of...unconventional, like the donor catalog and bank, pretty much guarantees...speculation and gossip."

A blast of wind hit them as they stepped outside. Shuddering from the cold, Brenna clutched the sides of her coat together.

"Come on, my car's right down there." Luke pointed to his enormous black Dodge Durango truck parked along the curb, almost directly in front of the courthouse.

He took Brenna's arm and walked her through the wind to his truck. She ducked her head, letting him guide her, the cold air stinging her eyes, making them tear. Moments later she was seated in the front passenger seat while Luke revved up the engine.

"Isn't this spot reserved for a VIP or something? How did you park here without getting ticketed?" Brenna flexed her icy fingers, pulling on her knit gloves. "Yesterday they told us to park two blocks down—if we could find a place in the free lot there. Otherwise, we were on our own and good luck."

She zipped up her coat just as the heater began to work, quickly warming the interior.

"One of my cousins is a cop," explained Luke. "He

suggested this spot and said he'd pass the word that my truck was right where it should be.''

''I thought your relatives didn't like you—except for your favorite aunt who enjoys grisly murders.''

''Well, some of the younger cousins, especially the guys, think I'm cool.'' Luke swung the truck into the sparse flow of traffic. ''And I shamelessly buy their friendship by taking them out to lunch or dinner or whatever.''

''Are you trying to get back in your family's good graces?'' Brenna asked curiously. ''Is that why you came back here after…'' Her voice trailed off.

''After my brother fired me and my family told me I was insufferable and full of myself, a sleazy showboat, and a vain big shot who was in danger of losing my immortal soul?'' Luke chuckled wryly. ''Mixed metaphors don't bother the Minteers, and they freely fling them.''

''But why—'' Brenna stared out the window. ''Where are we going?''

''To lunch, remember? We have a little less than an hour.''

''I'm not going to your place in…in the mountains!'' Her voice rose in panic. ''Let me out right now!''

''I'm not going home. You were right, there's not enough time.'' Luke cast her an inquisitive glance. ''You're scared,'' he observed thoughtfully. ''Of me?''

''I admit that I do have issues with being taken somewhere against my will by a man I hardly know,'' Brenna replied tersely.

''Issues,'' he scoffed, his dark brows narrowing. ''The current buzzword. An annoying one, too. Nobody has problems anymore, everybody has issues. Although it seems to me what you really have going on is an overload of hormones. You were operating in high maternal-protection mode.''

''Maybe so.'' Brenna folded her arms and rested them

on the shelf of her belly. She tried to will her pounding heart into beating a little slower.

"Were you freaked when I touched your belly in the courtroom earlier?" Luke blurted out. A flush of heat spread up his neck to his face. "I didn't intend to scare you, but when I saw the baby moving, it—I—"

"It's happened to me before," she said briskly. "People wanting to touch my belly to feel the baby move, except it's always been elderly women, and they always ask."

Once again she tamped down the swell of feelings the touch of his big hand on her belly had elicited within her. They meant nothing; they were a physiological reaction, she reminded herself. Insisted to herself. Hormonal overload and nothing else.

"It really was an irresistible impulse," explained Luke. "You see, I have a scene in my new book where a pregnant woman—"

"You're not going to have a pregnant woman murdered by a serial killer?" Brenna was aghast.

"No, but the killer does touch the pregnant woman's belly. It's very, very suspenseful. I want the reader literally shaking and screaming at the killer, 'Don't you dare hurt that mother and child.' And when he doesn't, the reader's relief will be—"

"You never did say where we're going," Brenna cut in sharply. He'd been exploring the mind-set of his serial killer character when he'd touched her? She shuddered.

"I'm kidnapping you to the China Palace, a few blocks from here. Ever been there?"

"Yes. And jokes about kidnapping aren't funny."

"That's what the homicide detective said to the serial killer in my first book," joked Luke. She didn't smile, and he sighed. "Well, the humor worked in the scene in the book."

"I'll take your word for it."

"I guess you'll have to, since you never intend to read a word I write. Okay, we'll move on to a neutral topic. The China Palace. It's owned by the Lo family, who ran a successful place in Philadelphia but moved here because they wanted to try a small town for a change. They're very strong supporters of my brother. Held a fund-raising dinner for Matt right here in the restaurant."

Luke pulled into the parking lot of the China Palace. Inside, the hostess and a waitress, both young Chinese women, greeted Luke enthusiastically and escorted them to a choice table by the window.

It appeared that Matt wasn't the only Minteer to enjoy support here, Brenna noted. And the admiration appeared to be mutual. Luke chatted and joked with the two young women as Brenna seated herself and opened the menu.

"Okay, which one are you?" asked one of the young women, finally acknowledging Brenna's presence.

It took Brenna a moment to realize that she was the one being addressed. And she had no idea what the answer to that question might be. She stared at Luke, baffled.

"Jennifer wants to know which one of the many Minteers you are," he explained, toying with a salt shaker.

"One of the sisters or one of the cousins?" prompted Jennifer, smiling invitingly at Luke.

Brenna met Luke's eyes. He shrugged. "I'll let you decide since you're the fiction writer," she said dryly.

Luke cleared his throat. "Actually, she isn't a Minteer. This is Brenna Morgan. Brenna, meet the Lo sisters, Jennifer and Isabelle."

"Hello," Brenna offered politely.

The Lo sisters gaped at her, barely managing to mutter a response before abruptly departing.

"What was that all about?" Luke frowned. "I've never known them to be rude before. I've been snubbed by plenty of people in this town but the Lo sisters have always been exceptionally friendly.''

"Yes, I noticed. And they weren't being rude, they were stunned." Brenna was amused. The astonishment on the Lo sisters' faces had been comical. "No doubt it was the shock of seeing you with a pregnant woman who wasn't related to you.''

"What are you implying?" Luke demanded.

"Me? Nothing.'' Brenna turned her attention back to the menu.

Luke looked over at the Lo sisters who were blatantly staring at him and Brenna. "I've been the object of enough gossip to know *that* particular look they're giving us," he muttered.

"I'm sure you have. I've heard some of the stories.'' Brenna never glanced up from the menu.

"For crying out loud, we're serving on a jury together. It's our lunch break!" exclaimed an aggrieved Luke. "And who told you stories about me? And, er, what were they?''

"When I told my neighbor that Congressman Minteer's brother was on the jury with me, she told me her brother knew you back in Harrisburg, in your pre-D.C. days.'' Brenna closed the menu. "I think I'll have a bowl of won-ton soup, an egg roll and chicken with cashews.''

"Who's your neighbor's brother?" pressed Luke.

"Steve Saraceni, the lobbyist."

"Uh-oh." Luke actually gulped. "Did she, um, go into specifics?''

"No.'' Brenna smiled sweetly.

"Well, it doesn't matter, anyway, because it's all ancient history, water over the dam. A place in the past we've passed out of.'' Luke paused to catch his breath. "Those days are over. Saraceni would say the same thing himself.''

Brenna sipped her water. "I'm so thirsty. The air in that courtroom is too dry.''

"Okay, the stories out of D.C. were even worse, I can't deny that." Luke fiddled with his napkin. "But that's—"

"Ancient history? Water over the dam? A place in the past you've—"

"Isabelle!" Luke stood up and waved the waitress over. "We're ready to order now."

Three

The afternoon session moved at a glacial pace, and several of the jurors had trouble staying awake. Brenna was one of them. Her eyelids felt heavy, keeping them open was an effort and a numbing lethargy spread through her.

It was too warm in here, the lawyers droned on and on, citing one dull legal reference after another. Plus, she'd eaten too much for lunch. The combination was narcotizing. She allowed herself to close her eyes. It would be all right to close them for just a moment.

Brenna drifted in the netherworld between sleep and wakefulness....

Images glided through her mind. She saw herself and Luke sitting at their table in the China Palace eating lunch. He used chopsticks—adeptly, too—while she and everybody else in the restaurant ate with plain old forks. Brenna smiled now, as she had then. She didn't know why, but his prowess with the Asian utensils amused her.

And then he'd put down his chopsticks and asked her quietly, "Why did you tell the truth about your pregnancy to me and nobody else?"

Brenna was faced with the very question she had asked herself when blurting out the truth she'd kept carefully guarded all these months. Why had she told Luke?

"I think it was because you were goading me," she'd replied slowly.

Luke nodded, seeming to accept the answer. Brenna was glad he did, but she didn't buy her own explanation. She should've dismissed Luke's speculations with a shrug, not caring what he thought. Instead, she'd told him her deepest secret. It made no sense at all, or else it made very revealing sense.

"What is the story you've told everybody else in town?" Luke demanded.

"Unlike you, I'm not too well known in this town, so everybody doesn't want to know about me. I did tell my neighbors and my doctor that I, uh, was in a relationship that didn't work out, and when I found out I was pregnant, the baby's father left."

"Which is exactly what I thought at first—until you emphatically informed me that there was no boyfriend," Luke reminded her. "Hasn't anybody else pushed for more details?"

"No. Nobody else has been that rude. Or pushy. Or intrusive. They've respected my privacy."

"Maybe they figured talking about it—about him, the supposed father—would upset you," surmised Luke. "Or maybe they just weren't interested enough to ask you anything more."

"Maybe," she'd agreed.

After that Luke had grown very quiet. He hadn't spoken much at all as they finished their meal and drove back to the courthouse, where he reclaimed the VIP parking spot for his truck again.

"We will now take a brief recess!"

The judge's stentorian tones plus the bang of his gavel startled Brenna back into full consciousness. Her eyes flew open, and she jerked forward. She felt a hand close over her upper arm, steadying her.

It was then she noticed how very close she was sitting to Luke. Their shoulders were touching, and she was leaning heavily against him. His hand was on her arm. Was she imagining it or was his thumb lightly stroking?

Brenna stood up as quickly as she could. Unsteady on her feet, she gripped the front rail for support.

"I...think I fell asleep," she murmured, running a hand through her hair.

"You and everybody else on the jury except Wanda and me." Luke rose to stand beside her. "Wanda has her knitting to keep her alert, and I'm used to sitting for long stretches while my mind wanders."

"Into serial killer land?" Brenna yawned, still drowsy.

"It's an interesting place to go. Although I was somewhere else this time." Frowning, Luke gripped her elbow. "Come on, let's go get a cold drink from one of those machines in the lounge."

She let him lead her into the jurors' lounge, where a TV set was tuned into the Weather Channel. The meteorologist was in a frenzy of excitement about a blizzard that was "crippling the plains." Scenes of blinding snow and abandoned cars along an interstate highway played on the screen.

"I wonder if they drag out the same old blizzard footage every time a new storm hits?" mused Luke, gazing at the television. "Who would know? All snowstorms look alike."

"As a devoted weather fan, that's blasphemy to my ears." Brenna sipped the cold soda from the can Luke had given her. "Thanks for this," she added.

"Consider it my contribution to the judicial system." Luke was flippant. "Keeping the jury alert and functioning is necessary to end this stupid trial as fast as possible."

"Then you can get back to creating murder and mayhem full-time."

"Yeah." He watched her sip the soda. "What do you do, full-time?"

"I draw."

He waited for her to elaborate. She didn't. She silently sipped the soda from the can, her eyes affixed to the blizzard on the television screen.

"Okay, I'll bite," Luke said at last. "What do you draw?"

"Mostly children and cute animals. I'm a freelance artist. I've illustrated children's books and magazines and drawn paper dolls and sketched children for sewing patterns and books."

"Has your work been published?" He looked startled. She nodded.

"And you earn enough to support yourself...and the baby?" Now he looked even more amazed.

His incredulity irked Brenna. Did she appear stupid? Incapable of possessing artistic talent? What was so unbelievable about her being paid for her work?

"Well, that's cool." Luke shrugged laconically, his surprise fading into indifference.

Which bugged her even more. "Oh, I'm glad you think so. I was worried you might find me *un*cool."

"Yeah, right." He laughed. "You couldn't care less what I think. And I like that too. You're...not boring."

"People who care about your opinion bore you? That sounds terribly jaded." Brenna tossed her empty soda can into the nearby trash bin, then walked over to the window and stared outside.

Moments later Luke again was by her side. "I am jaded," he said, resuming the conversation exactly where they'd left off. "Remember all those stories about me?"

"'Enough about me, let's talk about what you've heard about me'?" Brenna mocked.

Luke looked nonplussed. "I didn't say that."

"I understand subtext."

"Huh? What subtext? What are you talking about?"

"Never mind." Brenna turned and walked away from him.

Luke followed. It was as if he were on a leash and she held the end, dragging him along after her, wherever she went. The insight was appalling, yet he kept going, not stopping until he realized she was heading purposefully to the women's rest room.

She stayed there, not emerging until it was time to return to the courtroom.

Luke was already seated when she took in her chair in the box. She didn't look his way; she struck up a conversation with Wanda instead, admiring the colors in the afghan the older woman was knitting.

Luke found the discussion about yarn dull. He tried to enliven it. " All ready to hear more about those zany star-crossed lovers Amber and Brad?" he joked, interrupting.

"We're not supposed to discuss the case until deliberations." Brenna's tone was frosty, as if she didn't know he was kidding.

Luke knew she did. He heaved a deep, martyred sigh. "Brenna, I know you're mad, but—"

The judge entered the courtroom, and everybody rose in deferential silence. There were no more breaks until court was adjourned at four-thirty.

* * *

Later that evening Brenna was in her studio, an upstairs bedroom she planned to completely remodel someday. Right now it was empty except for her draft table and state-of-the-art desk chair, worth every cent she'd paid, considering how much time she spent in it. A ledge she had installed ran the length of one wall and held the tools of her trade, pens and pencils, both lead and colored, rulers and erasers, sable brushes, watercolors in every hue imaginable.

The lighting equipment had been another major expenditure, necessary to enable her to work at night, even though she preferred the natural sunlight of daytime. When the baby came, she might not be able to adhere to her normal routine of working all morning and afternoon. The baby would dictate her schedule, and that might mean working nights, when it was dark.

Brenna was prepared. Her new lighting made the room as bright as day.

Piles of books and magazines were stacked haphazardly around the room; getting shelves to put them on was another future project. An illustrated book of costumes lay open in front of her.

Brenna reached for a sharp yellow pencil to color in the loop-tied pigtails of the little girl with a turned-up nose and mischievous sparkle in her pale-blue eyes.

The little girl was six-year-old Kristin, who was wearing clothes in the style and colors that a child of that age in the year 1908 would have worn. Brenna had drawn Kristin's dress and bloomers, big ribbons and button shoes after researching her invaluable aid: *A Hundred Years of Children's Wear: 1850-1950.*

One of her favorite CDs, *Broadway Sings Happy,* a collection of peppy anthems from various shows, accompanied Brenna as she drew. Since that momentous day when she'd learned she was pregnant, Brenna had played nothing but upbeat music, songs about hope and love and laughter, songs that lifted her spirits. She firmly believed that maternal moods affected an unborn baby, and it was her duty to protect her child from any of her own less-than-positive emotions.

A boisterous rendition of "76 Trombones" filled the small house, and Brenna hummed along. When the telephone on the wall beside her began to ring, she picked up the portable receiver and tucked it under her chin while deftly coloring Kristin's hairbow a pale-pink.

"Oh, so you have a parade going on in there," said Cassie Walsh on the other end of the line. "That's why you haven't heard your doorbell ringing or the knocking—I mean, the *pounding*—on your door."

"Somebody's at my door?" Brenna quickly lowered the volume of her CD player.

The doorbell was ringing insistently, with some knocking—no, pounding was more descriptively correct—occurring at intermittent intervals. All the houses on the street had been built close together on small lots, enabling her neighbors to hear what she had blocked out with her music.

"Can you see who it is?" asked Brenna. She knew Cassie had a clear view of her front porch from the Walsh kitchen.

"It's a man," Cassie said. "That much I can tell, because it can't be a woman with that build. And if it is... Well, she has my deepest sympathy. You know, if you'd put your porch light on when it gets dark, I'd have a better view, Brenna."

There was a slight note of reprimand in her voice. Cassie had a younger sister and often fell into that role automatically with Brenna when it came to things like safety tips.

"Did I forget to put the porch light on again? Sorry, Cass. I guess I'm still not used to living in a house after a lifetime in apartments. Can you tell if it's a policeman?

Because I'm not opening my door to anyone else, and I'm not even sure I'll—''

"I'm sending Ray over there right now," Cassie said decisively and hung up.

Amid the ringing and pounding, Brenna crept quietly down the stairs. There were no windows in her small entrance foyer, and her door was solid oak, with no glass panes to reveal her presence to the person outside.

"I'm Ray Walsh and these are my boys, Brandon and Timmy." Through the door, Brenna heard Ray Walsh, Cassie's husband, the principal of the town high school. "We live next door. Can we help you?"

"I'm a friend of Brenna's, and I'm starting to get concerned. She isn't answering her door, and I know she must be in there. All the lights are on, and I could hear music playing a couple minutes earlier. I know she's inside—but maybe she can't get to the door?"

Brenna uttered a small astonished gasp. She also recognized that particular male voice. It was none other than her fellow juror, Luke Minteer.

And he was at her door? Why?

Automatically she opened the front door. A hard-blowing wind rushed into the house, and Brenna shuddered, rubbing her hands over her arms. Her long red maternity sweater, decorated with candy canes, wasn't enough protection against the cold night air.

"You are here!" Luke sounded triumphant.

His eyes met Brenna's, and their gazes locked.

"Hi, Mrs. Morgan," Brandon and Tim, both preteens, chorused.

Luke arched his brows sardonically, and Brenna quickly looked away from him, to greet the boys warmly.

"Thought we'd drop over and see what you're up to tonight, Brenna," said Ray. He tilted his head toward Luke.

"Friend of yours?" He left the option open for Brenna to confirm or deny.

"Yes, I know him." The breathlessness in her voice surprised her. She supposed it must be from the shock of cold air.

"Luke Minteer." Luke extended his hand to Ray and then to each boy. "Nice to meet you. It's good to know Brenna has such reliable neighbors," he added with a smooth sincerity that made Brenna's lips curve into a wry smile.

It wasn't hard to picture Luke out campaigning for his brother. He sounded as if he were chatting up potential voters right now.

"You're the writer, aren't you?" Ray eyed Luke thoughtfully. "And...the brother?"

Luke grinned. "Things are really starting to look up when I'm 'the writer' before 'the brother.' It used to be the other way around—I thought it always would be."

"Your book was amazing," Ray said eagerly, dropping his initial reserve. "Had me laughing one minute and on the edge of my scat the next. And the ending! *That* sure was unexpected! What a great read!"

"Thanks." Luke beamed. "I had to go to the mat to keep that ending. The editors wanted me to—"

"If you'll excuse me, I have to get back to work," Brenna injected. She started to close the door.

"Wait!" Luke stepped into the doorway, preventing her from shutting him out.

Brenna paused, her hand on the knob.

"Can I come in?" asked Luke.

She was certain he'd only asked because Ray and the kids were standing there. Otherwise, she had no doubt that he would've pushed his way inside without bothering to seek her permission. But since he had...

Brenna remained still, with the door partially closed and

Luke half in and half out, while she debated whether or not to let him inside.

Luke cleared his throat. "It's urgent, Brenna."

Another gust of wind delivered yet another icy wallop. It was too cold to stand there indefinitely. Brenna stepped aside, allowing Luke to enter.

"Brenna, if you need anything, give a call." Ray was already herding the boys from the porch. "I'm looking forward for your next book, Luke," he added with enthusiasm. "Don't make us wait too long for it."

Luke gave a friendly wave, then turned and closed the door behind him. "Nice guy," he remarked.

"And an admiring fan of yours." Brenna folded her arms, resting them on her belly. Inside her body, the baby had ceased its earlier gymnastics and was probably asleep. "If you want to continue your discussion with Ray, go on over. I'm sure he'll be delighted."

"I didn't come here to discuss my writing with your neighbor."

"Why *are* you here?" She eyed him warily.

Luke opened his jacket and slipped it off, tossing it toward the post of the wooden railing along the staircase. The hood snagged the top of the post and hung there.

"Sort of a slam dunk," he said with satisfaction. "Not bad, huh?"

"Let me guess—you played basketball in school?"

"High school," he confirmed. "Never made the team in college. Not, er, enough height, according to the coach."

She looked up at him. Flatfooted in her slipper-socks, it seemed she had to look way up. "I guess they only want those seven-foot-tall giants playing college ball."

"Yeah. If you're six feet tall—like me—you're out of luck." Luke squared his shoulders and looked even taller to her.

She noticed that he still had on the same clothes he'd

worn in court today, faded well-fitting jeans and the plaid flannel shirt, its colors muted, as if it had undergone repeated washings. She knew that the fabric was soft and warm because she had felt it against her cheek as she'd slept against him in the courtroom this afternoon.

The sensory memory hit her like a blast of frigid air, jolting her, making her feel a little dizzy. The breathlessness she'd originally attributed to the cold wind was back, which meant there had to be another cause for it.

This time Brenna didn't kid herself into believing it was anything other than his stunning sensual impact on her.

She gazed up at him, so male and tall and strong. So virile.

What was the line in that old, country song, something about "looking better than he had a right to"? Oh, that was Luke Minteer! And he was here in her house, staring down at her with his piercing Irish-blue eyes. She felt an unfamiliar melting warmth ooze through her, pooling deep in her belly.

Brenna gulped. "I know you're not here to discuss your ex-basketball career. You said it was urgent."

"I meant it was urgent that you make up your mind to let me in. I was freezing my, er, I was really getting cold standing out there." He rubbed his palms together. "Any coffee?"

"I don't drink it. I've never liked it. I have tea and hot chocolate," she added reluctantly. Was she obliged to offer hospitality to a drop-in visitor?

"No, thanks." Luke made a face as if she'd offered him rat poison. "Anyway, why I'm here...I know why you blew up at me in the courtroom today."

"I didn't blow up at you!"

"Figuratively speaking. Hey, you were mad, Brenna. Come on, admit it."

"I wasn't mad," she insisted. "I—" She broke off, then

began again. "I'm working this evening, Luke. I don't have time for guests."

"I'm not a guest. I just stopped by to tell you that I figured out what got you so riled this afternoon. It was because I didn't give you a chance to talk about your job." He wore the satisfied smile of one who has discovered an elusive truth. "I didn't mean to cut you off, but somehow—"

"The conversation got turned around to focus on you? Funny how that always seems to happen, isn't it? You do love talking about your favorite subject—you!" She was fighting hard to hold back a smile of her own. He was tangibly turning on the charm; she could feel it.

"And that made you mad, isn't that right, Brenna?"

"No, I was simply tired of talking to you, of talking about you, of listening to you."

She was particularly tired of the roller-coaster thrills being in his company provided her, but Brenna was not about to add that. Better to offend him by letting him believe she found him a tiresome bore. Because if he were to suspect these *feelings* he'd stirred up in her...

A pregnant woman, at the mercy of an overload of hormones, developing a schoolgirl crush on the town's bachelor rogue? Oh, it was too embarrassing to contemplate.

"Serving on a jury means enduring all the lawyers' blather, not the other jurors," she added baldly.

Luke gave a huff, his expression one of disbelief mingled with indignation. "Well, you don't have to worry, I won't continue to *bore* you. In fact, I'll spare you from having to endure any more of my...blather. From now on, I won't talk to you at all."

"That works for me," Brenna said glibly. "Good night."

"Good night!" He retrieved his jacket from the post. Brenna felt her baby awaken with a sudden thrust and begin to kick forcefully. She drew a sharp breath after a particularly enthusiastic strike.

Luke, his hand on the doorknob, had turned around in time to see her reaction.

"You flinched." He scowled. "Are you okay, or do you intend to go into labor right now?"

"I'm okay. Susannah or Simon's foot connected with one of my internal organs. A kidney, I think."

"Simon," Luke repeated, dropping his hand. "*Simon?* Don't tell you you're thinking of naming the kid Simon?"

"Only if it's a boy. If she's a girl, she'll be Susannah."

"Susannah is all right, I guess, but Simon as in 'Simple Simon Met a Pieman'? As in Simon Says? And that arch villain Simon Legree? You can't be serious."

"Simon is a wonderful name!" Brenna was defensive. "It's a classic, biblical and timeless. It's strong but stylish and not overused—"

"You sound as if you're quoting from one of those baby-name books. You can't take them seriously. Case in point, one of those books claims that Hortense is ripe for a comeback."

"Not one of the name books I've read says that," protested Brenna, "and, anyway, there is a world of difference between Simon and Hortense."

"The sperm donor was half-Swedish, so why not choose a Viking name? Might as well play up the kid's heritage, since it's the only thing he'll ever get from his father."

The implied criticism stung Brenna. "You were just on your way out the door, after promising you wouldn't talk to me anymore, remember?" she needled him.

Luke's mouth thinned into a straight line. "You can be really bitchy at times, Brenna."

"True. I can be. And a charming smooth operator like you doesn't have to put up with it. I'm sure this town is filled with nonbitchy types who would love it if you dropped in on them. So why don't you?'' She opened the front door and held it for him.

''That's a blatant invitation for me to leave,'' accused Luke.

''As blatant as I could make it,'' she agreed.

Cold air was beginning to fill the foyer again, thanks to the opened door. Brenna shivered.

''Why am I still here?'' Luke tossed out the question, glaring at her, as if challenging her to supply the answer. ''Why did I come over here in the first place?''

His eyes swept over her, taking in her defiant stance, her feet planted wide apart, one hand on her hip while her other hand kept pushing the door open wider, letting the wind blow inside. She was probably hoping a gust would blast him right out of the house.

To his extreme consternation, Luke couldn't decide if her aggressive posture infuriated him or turned him on. Or both.

Worse, he already knew the answers to the two questions he had posed, though he could only hope *she* didn't.

He was here because he couldn't stay away from her. Because the need to be with her had somehow overpowered his common sense and his willpower to stay away from her.

His mind had short-circuited this afternoon when he'd learned she was a successful artist, one who actually made a living from her work. He'd been impressed, and the odd vicarious pride that had streaked through him unnerved him. If he hadn't stopped himself, he would've deluged her with questions and given himself away. So he'd played it cool and *she'd* turned cold.

But instead of being relieved, all he could think about was how to make things right with her again. After staring blankly at his computer screen tonight for over two whole hours without typing a single word—his first-time-ever case of writer's block—he'd conceded that writing was a lost cause. His imagination had been taken over by Brenna Morgan!

It was as if he were possessed, so he'd hightailed it over here seeking exorcism. Her unwelcoming bitchiness, coupled with the sight of her in that absurd candy cane sweater, her belly swollen, her face pale without makeup, her hair tumbled around her shoulders in a tangled mess, should've done the trick.

He *should* have been cured, his clear thinking restored. He *should* have been able to go right home and write that scene where the serial killer touched the pregnant woman's belly, the one that he'd improvised on the spot today, after touching Brenna.

Instead, instead…

"Damn," Luke swore softly. "What have you done to me?"

He reached out and cupped her cheek with his hand. Her skin was soft and warm, and he lightly stroked it with his fingertips.

A moment later she backed away from him, her gray eyes flashing. "What are you doing?"

"Good question," murmured Luke. He moved swiftly to close the door, then leaned against it, his back chilled by the cool wood. "But the only answer I can come up with is that I'm not doing enough."

His arm snaked out and he seized her wrist with his hand.

Brenna stared down at his fingers manacling her wrist. "Don't, please!"

He heard the fear in her voice, and it called to mind her momentary panic in his car this afternoon, when she'd thought he was taking her to his house.

"Are you afraid of men in general or me in particular?" he asked quietly. He didn't loosen his hold on her wrist.

"Let me go." Brenna licked her lips, and he followed the movement of the tip of her tongue with avid eyes.

"I won't hurt you, Brenna." He slowly, gently, but inexorably pulled her toward him. "Don't be afraid of me."

"I'm not afraid!" she exclaimed fiercely. "I might have...issues...about being manhandled, but I'm not afraid!"

"Manhandle you? Never, honey. I'm known to have a slow hand." Luke chuckled softly. "A light touch."

She was only an inch or two away from him now. "Sounds like song lyrics to me," she said huskily.

He touched her cheek. "If you're not afraid of me, prove it, Brenna."

"By doing what?" Brenna's breathing was hard and fast, her pupils dilated wide.

With arousal, Luke was certain of that. Not fear, never that. She couldn't be afraid of him. He gave a tug, pulling her against him, as close as her pregnant belly would allow.

"I'll think of something," he said lazily, sliding both his hands to her hips.

"Have you lost your mind?" Brenna gaped at him. "I'm almost nine months pregnant, for godsakes!"

Four

"There can be no doubt about that," Luke agreed. "I actually can feel Susannah or Sam kicking." His blue eyes grew round as saucers. "What a weird sensation!"

"Try experiencing it from the inside, if you want weird," murmured Brenna, noting his renaming of her son.

"Thankfully, I'll never have to," Luke's relief sounded heartfelt. "Women are a helluva lot braver than men when it comes to certain things, and having a kid tops that list."

Brenna felt the grip of Luke's hands on her hips loosen as the baby's strongest kicks became noticeable to him. While he was distracted, she should take the opportunity to shove him away. She could make a dash into the downstairs bathroom, only a few feet away, lock herself in, open the window and scream for Cassie and Ray.

They would hear her, she knew. They would be over here within moments to rescue her.

So why didn't she do it? Brenna asked herself as Luke's

fingers tightened once more, keeping her right where she was.

"And it's Susannah or *Simon,* not Sam." Instead of escaping from him, she corrected him.

"We'll discuss that later." He widened his stance and settled her more intimately into the cradle of his thighs, then began to nuzzle the side of her neck.

His arousal pressed thick and hard against her. Brenna's heart began to pound against her ribs so wildly, she wondered if Luke could feel that, too. Yet her arms remained at her sides, and she made no attempt to push him away from her. Her uncharacteristic passivity shocked her.

"See." Luke's mouth blazed a trail of nibbling kisses to her ear. "Nothing to be scared of, Brenna." His lips traced the shape of her ear, and he carefully enunciated each word.

Brenna's hands slowly glided to his chest—to finally push him away, she thought. But they seemed to be operating of their own volition, because instead of giving Luke a hearty shove, her fingers curled around his jacket.

"I already said I'm not afraid of you," she whispered.

And she truly wasn't. Which would completely explain the mystery of why she felt no need to involve her neighbors in what was a very private matter. She neither needed nor wanted to be rescued. She hardly had time to process that insight when Luke's lips brushed lightly, sensuously over hers.

"Good." His warm breath, scented with an enticing mix of coffee and peppermint, flowed over her.

Brenna's head spun. What he was doing felt so good…everything did—the feel of his big hands anchoring her against him, her breasts crushed comfortably against the solid wall of his chest, his mouth so warm and seductive on hers.

Brenna quivered, clinging to him as an unfamiliar melting pleasure began to pervade her body. Her nipples, so sensitive during her pregnancy, tightened into taut points and began to tingle in the most disconcerting way.

She'd been aware of the changes in her breasts as her body prepared her to nurse her child, but the sensations evoked by the close contact with Luke's chest were brand-new. She wondered what it would feel like if he touched her there, with his fingers, with his mouth.

Brenna froze. These images and feelings, the wildness and the sensuality... They were overwhelming her; she couldn't handle it. What if she were to simply give in to them...?

I was overwhelmed and overpowered by my feelings, Brenna! I just couldn't help myself! Her mother's voice, girlish and plaintive yet subversively pleased, echoed in Brenna's head like a ghost from the past.

And Brenna's own silent response was the same as it had been when she'd been a child, listening to her mother's dramatic confessions. *But try to, Mom! If only you would at least try to fight the overwhelming, overpowering feelings.*

A futile wish, because Marly Morgan adored being at the mercy of her overpowering, overwhelming feelings; she thrived on being *helpless with passion,* her favorite dramatic description of her favorite state.

The very concept made Brenna cringe, then and now.

Her mother's perennial can't-help-myself excuse had inspired Brenna early on to control her impulses, her emotions, her wants. Even her needs. Brenna Morgan would not be overpowered or overwhelmed, she would not be made helpless by anything or anyone.

But here she was, on the verge of all those things—with Luke Minteer.

It seemed that it was time she took her own advice and at least *tried* to fight these overwhelming, overpowering feelings.

"What is it, honey?" Luke was attuned to her sudden emotional withdrawal, but he continued to hold her.

"This is just plain crazy. I'm not thinking straight." Brenna nearly wailed. "My common sense has…has been usurped by a hormonal blitz."

"Usurped, huh?" Luke gazed down at her, studying her delicate features, his eyes lingering on the alluring fullness of her lips. "There's a word that doesn't come up in everyday conversation. At least, not in mine."

"It's an effective word. And applicable." She lowered her eyes to avoid his intense scrutiny.

"Hmm, wonder if I can work it into the dialogue in the current chapter of my book?"

"Would that be between the killer and his victim of choice? Ugh!"

"Ah, my little muse. How did I ever manage to write without your invaluable guidance?"

Luke was on the right track, keeping it light and glib, Brenna thought, relieved. She would wisely follow his lead and defuse the emotional intensity building between them. Hopefully her common sense, which had gone missing when he touched her, would quickly return.

It occurred to her that moving out of his arms and away from him would be a considerable aid to that process. Instead, Brenna remained where she was. In his arms.

Despite her intentions, the syrupy warmth diffusing throughout her body made her feel too languid and lazy to do anything else. She decided she could be glib just as easily here as from across the room.

"A muse," she repeated. "You'll understand that I'm less than thrilled to be considered a muse who inspires horrific scenes like a serial killer terrifying a pregnant woman. Not to mention whatever awful scene you might dream up using the word *usurped*."

Luke laughed softly. "In other words, don't try to blame my nauseating sensationalist writing on you, Brenna?"

His words, his tone, were smooth and flip, but the way he was holding her—Brenna stole a quick look at his face and quickly averted her eyes again—and the way he was looking at her, was not.

The mixed signals confounded Brenna, but she played gamely along. "You took the words right out of my mouth, Luke."

"I'd like to put something *in* your mouth, honey. Are you going to let me?"

Brenna nearly choked.

They were definitely having two separate conversations on two different levels, the jokey spoken one, and the intense nonverbal one being conducted by their eyes, their hands, their bodies.

"You see, *you* have a hormonal blitz as your excuse." His tone was no longer quite so light and breezy. "So what's *mine*, Brenna? You might not believe this, but I've never put the moves on a pregnant woman before. "

"No?" *Keep it light, Brenna,* she silently repeated her mantra. "And here I was thinking you did this sort of thing all the time."

"You think I get some kind of kick out of, uh, being kicked by the baby within?"

"Not that I'm condemning you for that," she said, parroting his own words back to him. "I'm very open-minded."

"Don't, Brenna." Luke made a strangled sound that was something between a laugh and a groan. "Don't make me laugh. Don't make me…like you more than I do already. It's bad enough that I want you as much as I do."

"You want me," she repeated, the words affecting her viscerally.

Hearing him proclaim it was as potent as feeling the

physical evidence hard and insistent against her. That surprised her. She wouldn't have thought herself susceptible to sexual sweet talk—if that's what it was.

"You know I want you, Brenna. And we both know it's ridiculous." He sucked in a gulp of air, peering down into her wide gray eyes. "Don't we?"

"Yes," she agreed, nodding fervently. "Absolutely ridiculous."

"You should tell me to get lost. Pronto."

"Yes, I should. And I will."

"But not yet," he added quickly.

Too quickly, Luke acknowledged ruefully. She had to know how very much he didn't want to leave her. That would give her power over him, and he felt a pang of foreboding. During his political operative days he'd learned that ceding power to anyone for anything could be costly indeed. It was a lesson he'd mastered all too well, one that had stayed with him despite his career change. Or perhaps because of it.

What would be the cost of giving in to this urge to kiss her? Luke was shaken by how very badly he wanted to.

He could almost *feel* his normally dependable sharp and calculating mind getting derailed by the touch of her hands, the feel of her soft breasts pressed against him. Desire was a potent force, but one he was familiar with, one he could control. This was different.

Luke gazed at Brenna. He enjoyed talking to her, looking at her, simply holding her. Combined with this desire he felt for her...

How did a man resist that staggering, potent combination? To make matters more complicated, Brenna had fully agreed with him that their predicament was ridiculous, so he couldn't even argue with her—which he would've done, gladly, had she challenged him.

But she hadn't, thus giving him no grounds for a quarrel,

which would've created some head-clearing distance between them. Instead they remained close, on every level. Though she was nine months pregnant and they hadn't even kissed, the simple act of embracing her was fast transporting him to a higher high than any he'd previously experienced.

Could he ever remember feeling such desperate urgency, such aching need?

Heat surged through him like molten lava. What Brenna Morgan stirred in him was new, a most intoxicating thrill. He wanted to explore it further, to see where this subtle but powerful sensuality would lead. He held her even closer.

Brenna locked her arms around his neck, squirming against him, tormented by the unfamiliar, aching frustration of wanting but not having. Of being close but not nearly close enough. Of longing to let go but not daring to.

Was this what happened on the road to becoming helpless from passion? To being overpowered and overwhelmed to the point of not being responsible for her actions? For the first time, Brenna saw the seductive appeal in that excuse. And tried to fight it.

"Luke." She gasped his name. "Please! It's…it's too much."

"You've got it backward, sweetheart." His voice was as thick and husky as hers. "What you mean is, it's not enough. But we can remedy that. Right now."

His mouth took hers in a hungry, possessive kiss.

Brenna felt his tongue prod her lips and, reflexively, she opened them to him, allowing him entry to the moist warmth within. The intimacy was startling yet not alarming. Tempting and certainly not disgusting. All her previously held beliefs and fears of intimate contact seemed to be dissolving in the exciting fire of his kiss.

She felt his mouth moving over hers, evoking a fierce pleasure deep within her. His tongue touched hers, then rubbed seductively, invitingly, and she followed his lead, imitating his actions, returning the pressure of his lips, the thrust and parry of his tongue, with her own.

Pleasure and excitement and desire exploded inside her, obliterating a lifetime of caution and control, transforming it into aching, urgent need. She felt his big hand glide slowly upward to cup her breast and gently caress it, his thumb teasing the tip. The dual barriers of her sweater and sturdy cotton bra were no impediment to the electrifying effects of his touch.

Brenna moaned softly and arched into him.

"This is what you want, isn't it, honey?" he murmured hoarsely.

His hand moved again, under her sweater, over her bra, his fingers seeking and not finding a front clasp, and then nimbly undoing the double hooks in the back.

"I know it's what I want." He groaned the words as her swollen, unrestrained bare breasts filled his hands.

He fondled her, nuzzling her neck, rubbing against her as she whimpered, mindless with pleasure, clinging to him.

"I don't want to rush you or hurt you, Brenna." Luke slid his hand between her legs. "There has to be a way we can do this. We'll just have to be, uh, creative."

His words swirled in Brenna's head, but she hardly comprehended them. Her eyes were closed and she clung to Luke while her entire body reacted to the warm pressure of his hand. His fingers stroked her lightly, deftly through her leggings. Brenna knew he must feel the telltale moisture there, but she was too dazed to feel self-conscious or embarrassed.

Pleasure, extreme and intense, rocketed through her. She'd never known it could be this way, that she could feel like this.

And then, abruptly, the excitement turned frightening.

She was no longer standing! Luke had swept her up in

his arms. It was nothing less than terrifying not to touch the ground, to be held high against his chest, as if she were light as a doll instead of an almost-nine-months-pregnant woman, weighing the most she ever had in her life.

Reflexively, Brenna hung on to Luke, her arms tightly around his neck as he started toward the staircase.

"Where's your bedroom, honey? I'm guessing upstairs." His voice was deep and low, almost guttural.

The sound alarmed Brenna as much as her helplessness. The baby didn't like what was happening, either; she was sure of that. She felt the increased activity in her womb, as if Baby X were trying to kickbox the big intruder away from its mama.

The perception, whimsical though it might be, made Brenna tense. She knew all about children attempting to take care of helpless, foolish parents, having been such a child herself. No way was she going to be the mother of one. It was another promise she'd made to herself and to her unborn child—and one she intended to keep.

Starting right now.

"Put me down!" Her voice shook, sounding neither as forceful nor clear as it could have. As it *should* have!

No wonder Luke didn't take her command seriously. "It's okay, sweetie. You're not all that heavy."

He thought she was being polite, looking out for his well-being, saving him from lower back pain and strain! Brenna felt giddy laughter bubble up in her.

No one was more shocked than she when she burst into tears instead. And began to strike at him with her fists.

Her blows caught Luke off guard, though he ducked his head in time to miss getting smacked in the face.

"Brenna, what are you doing?" Luke stopped in his tracks halfway up the staircase.

His voice, stunned but not angry, jolted Brenna back to

the present. Aghast at her own violence, she stopped hitting, her fingers quickly uncurling.

"Brenna? Honey?" Luke stared down at her, concern replacing the desire and subsequent astonishment that had clouded his eyes. "What is it?"

"I asked you to put me down." To her mortification, a fresh flood of tears overtook her. Each word she spoke was punctuated with a sob. "And you...you didn't." She couldn't seem to stop crying.

"Oh, God, it's the baby, isn't it?" Instead of putting her down, Luke raced back down the stairs, carrying her into the small living room off the entrance foyer. He looked stricken as he gently laid her down onto the sofa.

"Are you in pain? Should I call the doctor? Yes, of course, I should. I will, right now!" He careened from the room, only to return a second later. "Who is your doctor? And where's the phone?"

Brenna sat up. He looked wild-eyed and panicked and was zooming around like a cartoon character. Clearly, he'd misunderstood her protest, and the entire situation suddenly struck her as hilarious. Not to mention absurd.

This time her laughter came as quickly as her tears had moments before.

Luke did not join in the merriment. "You're hysterical." He bent down and took both her hands in his. "Brenna, it's going to be all right, honey, I promise you."

Using his hands as leverage, Brenna pulled herself to her feet. She was calming down now, her emotions beginning to level. The baby must have known it, because the frantic kickboxing slowed to mellow pokes.

"Sit down, Brenna," ordered Luke, trying to push her back down onto the sofa. "Better yet, lie down. I'll call the doctor and we—"

"I don't need a doctor, Luke." This time her voice held all the clarity and strength it had lacked during the debacle on the stairs. "I just want you to leave. Immediately." Her tone also possessed the steely, icy edge she had honed to perfection over the years.

It was one that Luke had never heard from her, and it visibly affected him. He stared at her, uncertain and uneasy.

"Brenna, what happened tonight—"

"Won't happen again, Luke. Not ever." She hoped she sounded threatening enough to be taken seriously. "Get out of my house and leave me alone. I'll...I'll make you very sorry if you don't."

It worked! She must've sounded as menacing as a henchman working for the Sopranos, because Luke strode from the room and out the front door without a backward glance.

Brenna sank slowly back onto the sofa and rested her elbows on her knees, her head in her hands.

She sat there, consumed by memories of the inexplicable, terrifying and wondrous passion that Luke Minteer had evoked in her. And that she had evoked in him?

Brenna wasn't sure. After all, he had a reputation with women, and for all she knew any available, willing female might turn him on—despite his claim that he didn't, as a rule, fancy pregnant women.

Well, she'd been willing—at least for a short while there—but she would never, ever be available to him or to any other man. Brenna thought of her mother's terrible relationships with all the wrong men and, finally, with the man who had committed the one act not even Marly Morgan could excuse.

"Brenna!"

Cassie Walsh's voice startled Brenna from her increasingly disturbing reverie.

Brenna jerked her head up and stared in astonishment at her neighbor, standing in front of her.

Cassie sat down beside her. "I heard Luke Minteer peeling rubber, racing out of here like a speed demon at about a hundred miles an hour.'' Cassie was thoroughly disapproving.

''So you came over here to see if the reason he writes so successfully about serial killers is because he happens to be one?'' Brenna managed a wavering smile. ''I'm fine, Cassie.''

''Your front door was unlocked.'' Cassie put a sisterly arm around Brenna's shoulders. ''And you've been crying, Brenna.''

Brenna touched her fingers to her cheeks, which were still wet with tears. She'd almost forgotten she had cried. And in front of Luke Minteer! Since she never cried in front of anybody, the act seemed as intimate as…Luke's touch. As her responses to him.

Brenna heaved a soft groan. What an embarrassing, unnerving mess this was! How could she ever face Luke in the courtroom tomorrow?

Maybe she could call in sick. Surely her doctor would vouch for her if she were to tell him she was feeling ill and needed to stay at home in bed. Weren't there alternate jurors available to fill in for such emergencies?

''Brenna, I want you to know that you can trust me.'' Cassie was looking at her with concern and speculation. ''I mean, we've only known each other since you moved in last year, but I think we've become really good friends and—''

''We *have* become really good friends, Cassie,'' Brenna agreed, interrupting. ''And I'm so grateful to have you and Ray and the kids living next door as neighbors and friends.''

Cassie leaned forward attentively, as if prompting Brenna to continue. But Brenna had nothing more to say. The two sat in silence for a few moments, and then Cassie rose to her feet.

"Well, I guess as long as you're okay, Brenna..." Her voice trailed off.

"I am, Cassie. Honest. And thanks for checking up on me," Brenna added with a smile. "It's nice to know somebody cares about us." She patted her swollen belly. The baby was quiet now. "About Susannah or Simon and me."

To Brenna's surprise, Cassie's eyes misted with tears. "Brenna, we do care. And I have more than an inkling of what you're facing. I was a single mother myself for a number of years."

"You were?" Brenna was surprised. The Walsh family seemed like such a close, tight-knit unit, the type of family who'd always been together.

Cassie nodded her head. "My first husband left me and the boys when they were just babies. That was a really rough time. I took Tim and Brandon home to live with my parents and grandmother and my sister. I don't know what we would've done without them. But you don't have a family to fall back on, Brenna."

"No, but don't worry about me, Cassie." Brenna didn't bother to add that basically she'd been on her own for years. Having someone "to fall back on" was an alien concept.

Brenna Morgan depended on herself.

"I'm fine," she reiterated.

"You always say you're fine." Cassie frowned. "Even if you weren't, you wouldn't admit it. But, Brenna, you and your baby need family, you need—"

"How about if you and Ray and the kids are my honorary family?" Brenna suggested brightly. "There couldn't be a better family to have than you Walshes." She paused. "I never knew Ray wasn't the boys' real dad, Cassie. He treats them the way he treats little Abby. Just like his own."

"He legally adopted the boys right after we were married. And now they are his own kids in every way, just like Abigail.''

"Ray is a wonderful man," Brenna said warmly. "It's good to know guys like him actually exist in real life."

"Yes." Cassie's face darkened. "Unfortunately, good-for-nothing jerks who contribute nothing but their genes to the next generation also exist in real life. You can't imagine how much I detest men who shirk their duties as a father, the…the emotional and financial obligations that each and every father *owes* to his child. To just opt out, to blithely assume the mother will handle everything… It makes my blood boil, Brenna!''

Brenna assumed that Cassie was thinking about her sons' biological father, who must have been one of those detestable shirkers. She wasn't sure how to reply. To bash Cassie's ex or to praise Ray Walsh again?

She tried to do a little of both. "Some men are responsible and kind, and others aren't." Brenna gave a philosophical shrug. "That's just the way it is, I guess."

"There has to be a better way," Cassie muttered fiercely as Brenna walked her to the door. "*Somebody* has to do *something* to make things better for mothers and children."

"I guess garnisheeing men's wages to pay child support is a step in the right direction, at least financially," remarked Brenna.

"And we have that law in Pennsylvania. Think about it, Brenna. At the very least, your baby deserves its father's financial support."

Brenna thought of the medical student who didn't even know he was going to be a father, though his contribution had enabled her to be blessed with this wonderful gift of a child.

"It doesn't matter to me. I know I'm very fortunate to be able to support my baby all by myself," she assured Cassie.

Cassie did not appear reassured as she left Brenna's house for her own. She looked furious, no doubt still enraged by the heartless abandonment of her sons by their birth father. Brenna considered calling Cassie back, to urge her to put the disturbing memories of the past behind her.

It was the best way to get on with your life after something bad had happened to you, Brenna knew. It was what she had done herself.

Except every now and then those bad memories would boomerang into your new, good life. Flashbacks—a not uncommon symptom of post-traumatic stress, so she'd been told.

Brenna swallowed hard. Undoubtedly that's what had happened to her tonight, when she'd been assailed by terror as Luke attempted to carry her up the stairs.

His size and strength and her own vulnerability to it triggered her panic. And though the circumstances tonight couldn't have been more different from—*that night*—her reaction, so deeply ingrained from *that night's* trauma, had been the same.

She'd pleaded and cried and tried to physically fight back.

To no avail, back then. But tonight she hadn't been harmed. She had won.

Or had she? Was it winning when there was no fight? Luke hadn't used his strength against her, he hadn't been trying to hurt her. Or to scare her.

But she'd certainly scared him! Brenna thought of Luke's own panic in response to hers and couldn't help but smile a little. He'd feared she was going into labor and had morphed into a stereotypical, nervous expectant father, a sitcom staple.

It was rather dear of him to be so concerned, especially since he wasn't the father, she decided.

And then she remembered how cold she had been to him

while he raced around wanting to help her. She hadn't been able to appreciate his motives at the time, not when she was still in the fearful grip of past threats.

So she'd driven Luke away with her words and her tone. He had left immediately, undoubtedly glad to be away from such a moody irrational shrew, and who could blame him?

Brenna certainly didn't.

After all, she wasn't looking for a good man like Ray Walsh to come along and take care of her and her baby— not that Luke Minteer had been auditioning for the role.

Why *had* he come over tonight, anyway? The longer she sat here thinking about tonight's strange events, the more Luke's actual reason for dropping in eluded her. Hadn't he mentioned something about her being angry with him at the courthouse this afternoon because he'd expressed no interest in her job?

As if he cared about either—her anger or her job!

As for him wanting to make love to her...

Now that she was firmly back in her right mind, Luke's professed desire for her was beyond comprehension. Why, how, could he want her in her current condition, her body swollen with child? A child who wasn't even his own.

She preferred not to think of her desire for him. There was only so much confusion a person's mind could deal with at any given time.

Brenna gingerly rose to her feet and slowly climbed the stairs to her studio. The partially colored-in figure of mischievous little Kristin, surrounded by her 1908 clothes and playthings, lay on the desk before her.

With considerable relief, Brenna picked up a pencil and got back to work.

When the phone rang fifteen minutes later, Brenna ignored it. Though it was a bit late for telemarketers, some ambitious ones had probably extended their calling hours. The answering machine would take care of that.

After six rings, she heard her own voice politely recite her recorded message, inviting whoever to leave a name and number. Telemarketers never accepted the invitation.

"Pick up. I know you're there, Brenna." Luke's voice boomed into the machine. "I know you're screening your calls."

Disconcerted, Brenna dropped her pencil. As always, while working, she'd been too absorbed to think about anything but the characters and their lives she was creating with her drawings. It put her into another world, which was her refuge, her escape.

And now Luke Minteer had invaded that private, peaceful place by crashing back into her consciousness.

He wasn't welcome. She had come up here expressly to work—and to avoid all thoughts of Luke Minteer. Now, here was his voice, filling her studio. Filling her head!

"If this machine cuts me off before you pick up, I'll simply call back, Brenna. I'm relentless about getting through to people who are trying to dodge my calls. I never give up. It was one of my greatest talents as a political hatchetman."

Brenna found herself smiling in spite of herself. She'd never heard anyone admit to being a hatchetman. In her experience, people tried to sugarcoat their less-than-admirable traits and deeds. Or deny them completely.

The machine clicked off, and the studio was quiet. For a moment. Then the phone rang again, and this time Brenna picked it up.

"I knew you were there," said Luke.

"Congratulations. Your record of getting through to people trying to dodge your calls still stands."

There was a split second of silence.

"I also considered the art of ironic distance to be another specialty of mine," Luke said wryly. "But you're as good at it as I am. Maybe even better."

"I'm not sure you mean that as a compliment."

"I don't. It just occurred to me how annoying ironic distance really is. Tiring, too."

"Well, since we're both annoyed and tired of each other, let's hang up and pretend that—" she gulped for breath "—that none of this ever happened."

"I can't forget, Brenna. I terrified you tonight, and I'm sorry." There was no flippancy, no ironic detachment in his tone now. He sounded genuinely concerned and contrite.

Brenna winced. "Don't, Luke."

"Don't what, Brenna? Don't apologize? Don't think about what you—"

"Yes, don't think about me," she cut in eagerly. "Think about *you*. About how furious you were when you left here."

"You don't get it, do you?" Luke heaved a long sigh. "Do you know why I left when I did, Brenna?"

"Of course. Because I kicked you out. And off you went—at about a hundred miles an hour, according to my neighbors."

"Brenna, the reason why I left so abruptly had nothing to do with you kicking me out. In fact, it's impossible to kick me out. Just ask anybody who's ever tried. When ordered to leave, I take it as a challenge and deliberately stay put. Needless to say, it irritates the hell out of people."

"Another one of your valuable talents, no doubt?"

"Unquestionably."

"I can see that politics' loss is publishing's gain," Brenna cracked.

"Brenna, listen to me," Luke's tone grew serious once again. "I left tonight because you were extremely upset, and I knew if I stayed, it would only make things worse for you. I had to go when you ordered me to, because if I didn't get out right then and there, I would've scared you even more. I didn't want to hurt or scare you, Brenna. I realized that you had to know you were in control of the situation.''

Brenna stared uneasily into space, discomfited. Luke had analyzed the situation—and *her*—a bit too accurately. Not that she would tell him so.

"*All* women want men to…to leave them alone when they say so," she pointed out. "It's why there are stalking laws."

"Brenna, I know it's more than that. I've been doing a lot of thinking about this. Something bad happened to you, didn't it, Brenna? Something involving a man, or—" there was an audible gulp from him "—men?"

Brenna closed her eyes. His voice was quiet and low, with understanding, with concern. It washed over her like a warm, soothing wave.

"Brenna?"

She had a sudden vital urge to pour out the story of that long-ago terrible night, but she fought against it. The very few times she'd ever talked about it had elicited what she didn't want. Pity.

She didn't need pity; she knew it could only be detrimental to her. Brenna well remembered the frequent bouts of self-pity her mother had indulged in, and look where *she'd* ended up!

As if he could see her across the telephone line, Brenna straightened her shoulders and lifted her chin to convey her resolve.

"Yes, something bad happened to me," she said brusquely. "But it was years ago, in the…the distant past. It's over, so let's just leave it at that."

She heard Luke's sharp intake of breath. "Brenna, you…you didn't have a…a run-in with a serial killer, did you? Or…or someone you loved wasn't murdered by one?'' He sounded completely shaken, ready to hit the ground from sheer horror.

Brenna couldn't help herself. She started to laugh. ''No wonder you decided to write crime fiction! You do have the imagination for it. No, I've never crossed paths with a serial killer, and I've never met anyone who has. Thank the good Lord for that.''

It took her a moment before she noticed that Luke was not sharing her amusement. There was no laughter, only silence, on his end of the line.

Brenna felt a pang of remorse. ''Luke, I'm sorry for laughing at your, um, kind concern but it was just so—''

''Serial killers aside, something bad happened to you and it involved a man,'' Luke said quietly. ''You admitted as much, and I can't find that funny, Brenna.''

She waited for him to press for details. When he didn't, when the silence on his end continued, she relaxed. ''I know this is probably the last thing a cool rogue type like you wants to hear, but you're basically a nice guy, Luke Minteer.''

''There was a time when that description of me would've been like a knife in the gut, back when I was intent on being the coolest rogue of rogues.'' Luke's laugh was self-mocking, without mirth. ''But now, being called a nice guy…well, it doesn't sound all that bad.''

''I'm glad. Because I…I appreciate your call tonight after…well, you know.'' Brenna couldn't bring herself to say any word to describe tonight's ''incident'' with Luke. She wasn't going to step into the landmine evoked by words like *kiss, touch, or passion.*

Luke must've known it, because he made no further reference to the ''incident'' either. ''I'll see you in court tomorrow for the next riveting installment in the Who Gets the Ring Saga,'' he said lightly.

''Yes.'' Thanks to this call, she no longer had to dread

seeing him tomorrow. She wouldn't have to fake an illness and pester her doctor for an alibi. That in itself was a relief.

But before hanging up, Brenna couldn't help adding, "Luke, let's not mention *it* tomorrow, okay?"

"You want to pretend *it* never happened. I hear you, Brenna."

"No hard feelings?" She was a bit surprised she even cared about Luke Minteer possibly harboring hard feelings against her.

"No hard feelings at all. After all, we're, uh, buddies, Brenna. Jury buddies, right?"

"Right." She smiled. "You really are a nice guy, Luke Minteer."

"Yeah, it's a well-kept secret, but I'm a gem. A modern-day Prince Charming. The kind of man a girl is proud to bring home to Mother. Shall I continue, or have I run the analogies into the ground?"

Brenna thought about that last one he'd mentioned. She wouldn't be bringing any man to meet her mother, and despite Luke's belief that he was some kind of rogue, Brenna knew that Marly Morgan would probably regard him as tame as a pussycat, as straitlaced as a Sunday school teacher.

Marly's tastes ran to what she described as "bad boys." Law enforcement had another term for them—felons.

Brenna shivered, remembering. And then, determinedly, she dismissed her dark thoughts.

"You'd better quit with the analogies, Luke," she said dryly. "You've not only run them into the ground, you've buried them six feet under."

"That's exactly what a snotty newspaper critic said about all the snappy similes in my first book. I guess I don't have to add that he isn't a fan of my writing."

"Oh, what does he know? The bestseller lists can't be wrong."

"Now you sound like my agent. Good night, Brenna."

Five

A snowstorm, complete with gray sky, icy wind and a blinding gust of flakes greeted Brenna when she opened her front door the next morning. Not for the first time, she wished for an attached garage to keep her car indoors, protected from the elements. Plus, she wouldn't have to endure winter's slap in the face first thing in the morning.

Brenna glanced longingly over at the Walsh house, where she knew the whole family was cozily ensconced for the day. According to the radio's list of closings, the entire school district was taking a snow day, citing frigid temperatures and the possibility of more snow later in the afternoon.

But court was in session. There had been no mention of the courthouse being closed in deference to the bad weather. Which meant she had to get herself there this wretched winter morning.

Mentally Brenna listed the tasks to be completed before

driving to the courthouse. Snow needed to be brushed from the windshield and the rest of the car windows; she probably needed to scrape off the inevitable buildup of ice, too.

Through the whirling snow, she could barely discern the outline of her car, parked along the sidewalk in front of her house.

The necessary tools were inside her car, and hopefully her key wouldn't freeze in the lock, as it had on similarly frigid days. That would mean a return trip to her kitchen for the small de-icer that Ray Walsh had so kindly given her after she'd had to borrow his a few times.

Brenna's head was lowered to spare her face and eyes from the bracing chill of the wind, so she didn't notice anyone coming up her front walk until a pair of hands closed over her shoulders.

She jerked up her head, and her eyes met Luke's. Somehow she must have intuited who it was before she saw him...because if she hadn't, Brenna knew she would have screamed.

Being grabbed unexpectedly had that effect on her.

"Let's go. I'm parked right in front of your car." Luke wrapped his arm around her, holding her close against him, using himself to shield her from the wind.

Moments later Brenna was packed into the passenger side of his big black SUV. The car was blissfully warm, the heat on full blast, the radio tuned to a fast-talking disc jockey who was making jokes about the latest celebrity arrest in New York City.

Luke slammed her door shut to walk around to his side, and for a moment Brenna was alone and enclosed in the warm quiet confines. Well, it would've been quiet, if only that DJ would shut up. Automatically she reached over and turned off the radio.

Luke climbed into the driver's side. "Hey, what happened to—"

"I can't stand that guy yammering in the morning—well, not at any time, actually. The other local station will have weather and traffic updates," she added helpfully.

"Stating the obvious. Like we can't see for ourselves that it's snowing, and traffic is going to be hopeless."

Luke didn't turn the radio back on, and Brenna was pleased until it occurred to her that she really had no grounds to take command of the airwaves while in his vehicle. The particular "shock jock" whom she abhorred had a lot of devoted listeners; Luke might very well be one of them.

She felt guilty, disturbing his morning routine. "Do you want me to turn the radio back on to—"

"Nah, leave it off." He pulled into a deserted, snow-covered street that was lined with the residents' parked, snow-covered cars. "Looks like everybody is staying home today."

Brenna nodded. "The school district called off classes and most businesses are shut down for the day."

"But there's no such break for us worthy citizens serving in the courthouse. They must figure the wheels of justice are equipped with snow tires and chains."

"Maybe trials are supposed to be like the mail. You know, going on through rain and hail or sleet and snow," suggested Brenna. "Remember that old jingle?"

"How could I forget it? My great-uncle Marty the mailman used to quote it endlessly. Uh-oh."

As he pulled up to a stop sign at a four-way intersection, they watched a car skid, nearly sliding into another car, which managed to swing out of its path at just the right moment.

Brenna expelled a nervous breath. "The roads are bad," she murmured. Unfortunately, she identified with the skidding driver, not the artful dodger.

"The trucks are out plowing and salting the main highways first. By the time they get to these little neighborhood streets—no doubt in the spring   the stuff will have melted on its own.''

She had to smile at his hyperbole. ''They're not quite *that* slow.''

''Creative enhancement, as we in the political arena liked to call outright lying. Has a much more positive connotation.''

Brenna was back to staring anxiously at the snow and skidding motorists. ''I don't remember them predicting snow for us yesterday. Of course, I didn't watch the eleven o'clock news with the weather report.''

''I did, so I knew it was coming. The Midwest blizzard moved faster than anybody thought it would. I thought you were the Weather Channel junkie. How could a snowstorm catch you unaware?''

''I was working till past midnight and didn't even have the TV on,'' Brenna admitted.

''Do you have to have complete silence to work?'' he asked curiously.

''No, I play music.'' Brenna thought of her show tunes, which never failed to touch her, to uplift her. ''I have lots of CDs and tapes of really lovely songs.''

''I *have* to have music while I'm writing. Total silence would drive me nuts. But I don't think my tastes would fall into your 'lovely' category.'' Luke cast her a quick sly glance. ''That's your cue to make some wisecrack about Music to Create Murder and Mayhem by.''

''I've heard way too many jokes about my love for show tunes to dump on your music. Everybody is entitled to their own tastes .''

''Ah, the perfect carpool passenger. Sucking up to the driver. Next you'll say you tried to buy a copy of my book, but it was sold out at the bookstores,'' he added dryly.

''Perfect passengers don't take control of your radio,''

she reminded him. ''And you can count on me never buying your books, unless you switch to writing romance novels with a guaranteed happy ending.''

''Just the thought of that is more bone-chilling to me than this weather.''

''Your devoted readers probably feel the same way. I really do appreciate the ride this morning, Luke. I'm sure the jurors' parking lot won't be plowed yet, which would mean driving all over town trying to find somewhere else to park and—''

''Finding a place to park was the least of your troubles this morning, Brenna,'' Luke cut in bluntly. ''You could've easily slipped on the ice and fallen flat on your face. Or on the baby.''

''Actually, I hadn't thought of that.'' Brenna was surprised that she hadn't—and even more astonished that Luke *had*.

In fact, Luke had visualized that alarming possibility last night, when the weatherman on the local news had warned about the likelihood of snow this morning.

He'd made up his mind right then to pick her up and drive her to the courthouse this morning, if court was in session. Which, unfortunately for those having to brave the as-yet-untreated roads, it was.

Luke braked to a stop at a red light and stole a glance at Brenna, sitting quietly beside him. He wasn't one to enjoy silence—he equated it with boredom or awkwardness—but he felt neither bored nor awkward with Brenna.

He felt comfortable.

What was that quote his brother Matt used when describing his relationship with his wife, Kayla? Something about ''speaking in silence being the most intimate connection between people''?

Luke had never quite comprehended what on earth Matt meant. Now he felt he might have an inkling.

Were he and Brenna "speaking in silence"?

Or was he going totally nuts?

She must have felt him looking at her, because she turned her head and met his eyes. Her lips curved into a half smile.

"What?" she asked.

"What do you mean, 'what'?" Luke attempted to sound blasé. He wasn't sure he succeeded.

"You look as if you want to ask me something." Brenna's smile widened. "Well, go ahead. This is your car and I'm the grateful passenger."

Now that she'd brought it up, there was something he desperately wanted to ask her, something he'd been thinking about since last night. Something he had lain in bed ruminating over, long after he should have been asleep.

Luke took a deep breath. "When that…bad thing you mentioned last night happened to you, uh, were the police involved?" he blurted out. "Was the—for lack of a better term—the perp ever caught?"

Her smile instantly disappeared, like in a comic strip panel where a smile flipped upside down into a deep frown.

"I told you I don't want to talk about that." Her voice was as cold as the wind whipping the snow around outside. "I told you it happened in the distant past and it's long over. What part of that didn't you get?"

"You said I looked as if I wanted to ask you something." Luke was defensive. "You said to go ahead and ask. So I did."

She gave an impatient huff. "I thought you wanted to listen to that idiot on the radio. I thought you were going to ask whether I minded if you turned his show back on."

"So much for speaking in silence," muttered Luke.

As far as he and Brenna were concerned, their silence was spoken in two vastly disparate languages. Which was exactly as it should be, because there was no "intimate connection" between them.

There was no connection at all. His lack of sleep was getting to him, making him imagine all sorts of foolish things that had somehow gotten stuck in the grooves of his brain.

Defiantly Luke turned on the radio.

The DJ's voice filled the air. He was raucously proclaiming, between snorts and guffaws, that men want to get laid all the time, therefore making platonic friendship between the sexes impossible.

"Idiot!" snarled Luke and switched the radio off again.

Brenna stared at the windshield wipers, which were getting a heavy workout in the storm. Her hands rested on her huge swollen belly.

"You don't agree with him?" she asked impassively.

"That all men think about is getting laid?" he snapped. "No, I don't agree. We—I think about other things. Although you probably don't believe me because of what happened last night," he added testily.

"You promised you wouldn't mention that."

"Sorry. You have so many conversational taboos, it's hard to keep track of them all. Refresh my memory… exactly what am I allowed to talk to you about besides the weather?"

"Stick to the weather and we'll get along fine," she retorted.

They drove along in silence, a smoldering silence, complete with dueling glares. Every time Luke shot her one, she gave it right back to him.

His sense of humor began to get the best of him. Brenna Morgan could be as annoying as hell, but somehow she amused him, too. Her stubborn refusal to back down reminded him of his younger sisters, Anne Marie, Mary Catherine and Tiffany.

Those little hellions had always stood their ground—and still did, though they were all happily married now with little hellions of their own.

Not that he thought of Brenna as a little sister. He stole a quick glance at her. Did he?

Brenna caught his look. It wasn't a glare, so she didn't return it. "You stopped glaring at me. Are you over your snit?"

"I don't have snits. Only girly-men have snits."

"I'll probably regret asking this, but would you please describe what you consider to be girly-men?"

"Oh, you know, those hapless twits who can't hit a ball with a bat and are mocked at their company softball games. The ones who can't tie good strong knots so when they're moving or on vacation, their stuff flies off their cars or pickup trucks and ends up all over the road."

"No wonder the poor souls have snits," Brenna said dryly. "They strike out at softball and are laughed at, their stuff gets strewn all over the highway and the drivers passing by are laughing and calling them girly-man."

"True."

"Actually, that's a useful bit of information, Luke. If my baby is a boy, I'm going to make sure he can hit a ball and tie a strong knot."

"He'll thank you for it." Luke smiled. "And if you need any assistance, give me a call. Every Minteer male hits 'em out of the park and ties knots of steel."

"No doubt from the age of five," Brenna added, getting into the spirit.

"Three," corrected Luke, and they both laughed.

Luke turned onto the street where the courthouse was located. The usually crowded, bustling area was empty, every reserved VIP parking place in the front of the building unoccupied.

"Where is everybody?" murmured Brenna. She looked

at the dashboard clock. "It's normally packed around here at this time. Court should be starting shortly and—"

The sharp, wailing sound of a police siren abruptly silenced her.

Moments later a uniformed policeman leaned in the window Luke had opened on his side.

"Hey, Patrick, what's up?" Luke asked. "This place is as deserted as an Arctic outpost."

Brenna wondered if this was Luke's cousin, the policeman who'd authorized their special parking privileges.

"The courthouse is closed today, Luke," said Patrick. "Didn't you hear it on the radio or TV?"

"I sure as hell didn't!" Luke added a few choice expletives. "And I listened to the whole list, too. Took forever! I heard every school listed, every meeting, just about every store in the whole damn mall, but not a word about the courthouse being closed today!"

"Yeah, word didn't go out till late. The powers that be waited until fifteen minutes ago to officially cancel." Patrick heaved a disgusted sigh.

"Why?" demanded Luke.

"Packed schedule. There's a trial in every courtroom, including that double homicide at the gas station last summer. The judges and lawyers want to speed things along on account of the holidays coming up," explained Patrick. "But when nearly 90 percent of the jurors called the courthouse or police station saying they wouldn't be in... Well, there was no choice. Court is closed for the day. I'm here to tell the diehards who show up to go home. So far you're only the fourth diehard, Luke."

Luke groaned. "Go ahead and substitute moron for diehard, Pat. I deserve it, I should've known."

"We both should've guessed, just from looking out the window," interjected Brenna, willing to accept her share of the blame. "I mean, when you really think about it, is there any way that Wanda or Roger or the others would've ventured out in this, with or without an official cancellation?''

Patrick leaned his head farther into the car. He looked at Brenna, then an expression of undisguised astonishment crossed his face as his gaze lowered to her unmistakably pregnant shape.

''Who are you?'' he fairly gasped.

Brenna stifled a grin. Obviously, the sight of Luke Minteer in the company of a pregnant woman unrelated to him was as stunning to Officer Patrick as it had been to the Lo sisters in the China Palace.

''Brenna Morgan.'' Feeling devilish, she leaned over and offered her gloved hand for Patrick to shake, leaving him no choice but to stick his hand across Luke to grip hers.

''Patrick Minteer, Luke's cousin. Pleased to meet you, Brenna. You, um—'' he glanced furtively at his cousin, whose face was a half inch away from their handshake ''—a friend of Luke's?''

''I'll have to ask him.'' Brenna wondered at this strange impulse she had to tease Luke Minteer. But it was too irresistible not to give in to. ''Are we friends, Luke?''

Luke's reply was a fierce scowl.

Patrick immediately dropped Brenna's hand and withdrew from the window.

''Luke, be careful driving, okay? Better yet, stay off the roads today. Even a fender bender could be nasty with, er, her in her…her condition,'' Patrick added uneasily, heading back to the patrol car.

''We're free! I feel like a kid who just heard school's been canceled,'' Brenna exclaimed jubilantly.

Luke stared stonily ahead. ''Why did you do that?''

''Do what?''

'''Are we friends, Luke?''' He did a mocking, high-pitched imitation of her response to Patrick's question.

Brenna flushed. Suddenly her small joke didn't seem all that funny. Certainly, Luke found no humor in it. She felt embarrassed, defensive. "He asked me a question and I wasn't sure of the answer. I thought I'd ask you since I don't make a practice of lying—or you might prefer *creatively enhancing*—to police officers."

"Oh, so it would've been *lying* to say, 'Yes, I'm a friend of Luke's'?"

"Maybe," she snapped. "I don't know if you consider me a friend of yours or not."

"Well then, what about a simple 'We're serving on a jury together'? That is certainly the truth. No need to consult me on that."

"You're right. That's exactly what I should have said. I'm sorry I didn't, but never mind, I'll go set the record straight right now."

She unlocked the door and pushed it open. Wind and snow gusted into the interior.

"Brenna!" Luke reached over to grab her, but she had already stepped down onto the sidewalk.

She was surprisingly fast for an almost-nine-months-pregnant woman, and it certainly helped that the sidewalks had been salted. By the time Luke gathered his wits and clambered from his side of the vehicle, Brenna had reached the passenger side of the patrol car.

Patrick Minteer leaned across the seat and opened the door for her. "What can I do for you?" he asked warily.

"Officer Minteer, would you mind driving me home? Your cousin—"

"That's enough, Brenna." Luke was right behind her, his hands on her forearms, his body surrounding hers like a protective shell. "I don't know what stunt you're trying to pull but it—but I—"

"Let me go." Brenna began to struggle. "I want to go home."

"I'll take you home." Luke began to pull her away from the patrol car.

"No!" Brenna grabbed hold of the car door and hung on. "Don't bother. I wouldn't want you to inconvenience yourself for another minute on my behalf. Your cousin said he would give me a ride."

It suddenly occurred to her that the young policeman had not yet agreed to her request. "Will you please, Officer Minteer?"

"Of course," he agreed.

"Stay out of this, Patrick," growled Luke. "It has nothing to do with you."

"Yes, it does!" cried Brenna. "A police officer giving a ride to a juror falls into the category of official civic business or something like that."

She thrust herself forward with such force, she succeeded in loosening Luke's grasp on her. She would've landed face first in the front seat of the police car if Patrick hadn't reached up to catch her by her shoulders.

"Holy Mother of God, Luke, she almost fell! And in her condition!" Patrick was distressed. "What's going on with you two?"

"We're serving on a jury together," Brenna said through gritted teeth. "Nothing else is going on. We're strictly fellow jurors, right, Luke?"

She was kneeling in the front seat, firmly trapped between the Minteers. Patrick was in front of her, still clutching her shoulders; Luke was behind her, his hands on what would have been her waist. If she still had a waist.

"Will you both let go of me? I feel like a steak bone caught between two dogs!"

Patrick immediately dropped his hands, but Luke moved even closer to consolidate his hold, wrapping his arms around her abdomen, around the baby. She couldn't get

away from him if she tried—which she did, wriggling in-
effectually in his arms.

"I'm taking her home, Patrick," Luke announced. "I'll
get her out of your hair right now, figuratively speaking."
He flashed his cousin a charming smile. "Literally, I'll get
her out of your car."

"No!" Brenna's voice rose. "I said no. You can't let
him drag me away, Officer Minteer, or you'll be aiding and
abetting a…a kidnapping. One juror has no right to abduct
another juror."

Patrick Minteer looked uncertain, glancing from Brenna
to Luke, then back to meet Brenna's eyes again.

"Please, Patrick," she said softly, suddenly sure he had
decided to side with her.

Until Luke spoke again.

"Don't pay any attention to her, Patrick. She's too emotional to know what she's doing. Remember every time
Aunt Molly got pregnant…." Luke's voice trailed off.

Patrick instantly recoiled, returning to his place behind
the wheel. He adjusted his hat, which had been knocked
askew during the brief scuffle, and didn't look at Brenna
again.

"You've really, really, *really* done it this time, Luke."
The young officer gripped the steering wheel with both
hands. "Go on, take her home. But you know it won't end
here. Oh, wait, just wait till…" He groaned and shook his
head.

Luke half pulled, half carried Brenna back to the Dodge
Durango, still idling along the sidewalk, with both doors
wide open.

"Some policeman your cousin is!" she said crossly as
he packed her inside. "He actually let you take me away
against my will. I should file a complaint. And who is Aunt
Molly? Patrick looked totally spooked at the very mention
of her name."

Luke didn't answer until he'd pulled the SUV into the street and was heading away from the courthouse. "Aunt Molly had these, er, memorable mood swings—every time she got pregnant. Which was five times! All in all, they made an indelible impression on many of us Minteers."

"I'm sure. But why did you let your cousin believe that *I* was a hormonal basketcase?" argued Brenna. Never mind that she'd invoked that same argument to herself, about herself, while trying to rationalize her feelings for Luke Minteer. Brenna grimaced. Now was not the time for even more rationalizing! "I only did what you wanted," she insisted. "I told Patrick we were fellow jurors. Then you came roaring after me like some…some wild Neanderthal. What was that all about? Just who is the crazy one here?"

"You know I didn't want you to go running off in the middle of a blizzard to tell him anything," Luke said tightly. "And I did not roar like a Neanderthal."

"I beg to differ. Now take me home right now or I'll…I'll get out at the next red light and knock on somebody's door and ask them to call me a cab."

"Oh, that would fix me, wouldn't it, Brenna? You wandering around in a subzero blizzard knocking on doors, hoping to find a cabdriver insane enough to come out in this weather to drive you? Yeah, that would hurt me a lot more than it would hurt you—or your baby." He gave a disdainful huff. "You sound like a little brat threatening to hold your breath till you turn blue because you think that'll really punish the grown-ups."

Brenna was appalled. He was right, of course. Her juvenile threat wouldn't hurt him at all—but it would certainly do harm to herself and the baby. She leaned her head back against the headrest and wondered if she was becoming as wacky as the Minteers' fabled Aunt Molly.

Luke was silent, pretending to concentrate on driving through the storm. But he was a native of this area and had driven through far worse storms, so he had ample opportunity to think while navigating the roads, to reflect on the staggering fact that yes, Brenna Morgan had hit exactly on the best way to punish him.

The image of her running away from him to roam through the frigid snow-blinding streets was as horrifying as the most heart-stopping murder scene he'd ever written. More so, in fact. His fictional creations and their fate had no power over him; he didn't care if an imaginary killer offed an imaginary victim.

But Brenna…oh, she had power over him. There was no use denying it when the possibility of something happening to her—even as stupid and unlikely as her bratty little threat—could unsettle him this way.

He switched on the radio, as much to hear the latest storm updates as to try to distract himself from his disturbing insight.

She was bad news, he lectured himself sternly. She was every "must avoid" he had ever warned or been warned about.

"This just in!" exclaimed an eager newscaster. "A giant old pin oak tree was uprooted by the wind and ice and has fallen across a portion of Route 128, knocking down power lines. Both the tree and the live wires are blocking the road, and 128 is closed indefinitely so crews can begin the removal and repairs. Motorist are advised—"

"Ah, this day keeps getting better and better." Disgusted, Luke turned off the radio. "I can't get home if 128 is closed. It's the only road that leads to Mountainview Trail, where I live. And even if I could get there, I'll have no power till they get the lines back up."

A moment of dark humor struck him. Well, at least he had something else to think about besides Brenna Morgan. He could now dwell on the massive inconvenience of no electricity and no way home.

"What will you do?" It was the first time Brenna had spoken since issuing her threat. She had been sitting in chastened silence ever since.

"Maybe I'll run the blockade and try to jump the oak and the live wires. That always seems to work in the movies." Luke turned the corner onto her street. "Just kidding."

"I'm glad you clarified that." She arched her brows wryly. "It wasn't too hard to imagine you trying it."

"Yeah, we roaring Neanderthals often do double duty as foolhardy stuntmen."

Brenna caught her lower lip between her teeth. "You weren't being a Neanderthal. I was out of line, the whole time." She swallowed hard. " And I...I apologize, Luke."

Luke frowned. How was he supposed to demonize her when she apologized to him in that sad little voice, with confusion all over her sweet face? How could he focus on everything that was maddening about her while her pretty white teeth worried the soft pink fullness of her lips?

At this rate, how was he ever going to convince himself he couldn't stand her, that he would rather be anywhere than around her?

"I was out of line, too," he said grimly. "The Aunt Molly comparison was uncalled for. Unfair." He heaved a sigh. "Untrue. Sorry."

Their truce silenced both of them once more, until they pulled in front of her house.

"Looks like you've got some friendly neighborhood helpers." Luke pointed his thumb at the two young boys, bundled heartily against the elements, who were shoveling her walk.

"Brandon and Timmy Walsh. Their mom makes them shovel my walk and dig my car out every time it snows, but she refuses to let me pay them. So I slip them money on the sly. I really think I ought to pay them for doing all that work.'' Brenna frowned thoughtfully. ''Do you think I'm sabotaging Cassie by—''

''No, because I agree with you. The only snow shoveling I did for free as a kid was for my parents and grandparents, and that was out of sheer self-preservation. They would've brained me with the shovel if I'd dare to ask them for money. The neighbors all paid me for my work. And look what a model citizen I grew up to be,'' he added cheekily.

''Well, actually, that's true. You serve when jury duty calls, you don't cheat on your taxes. Um, do you?''

''No way. One credo I've always lived by, even at my political operative worst—or best some might argue—was Don't Mess with the IRS.''

He braked the SUV to a stop, and Brenna reached for the door handle.

''Stay there. Let me get that for you,'' Luke ordered, jumping out to come around to her side and open the door.

Luke lifted her down, and this time there was no mutual fury to mask the effects of their proximity to each other, as in the police car just a short while ago.

This time their gazes met, their bodies touched, and the heat that rose between them was steamy enough to melt the blustery snow.

''Hi, Mrs. Morgan!'' bellowed Timmy, waving his arm.

The intensity was broken, for at least a second or two. Then Luke took Brenna's arm to walk her to her door, and their closeness catapulted them back under the spell of their attraction.

''Was the 'Mrs. Morgan' bit their mother's idea?'' murmured Luke, leaning down to speak softly into her ear.

So the children wouldn't hear. But mainly because he couldn't resist the temptation of touching his lips to her delicate earlobe.

''Yes. Cassie thought with the baby coming and all...'' Brenna paused to breathe. It was freezing cold, but she felt as if she were on fire with a raging fever. "Cassie thought the *Mrs.* would be easier for them to understand," she added breathlessly.

"She means easier for her to explain to them. Around here a divorce is far more respectable than a deliberate foray into single parenthood."

His breath warmed the icy tips of her ears. "P-prob-ably," she agreed, feeling weak.

They walked on the cleared pavement, approaching the two boys.

"Mrs. Morgan, you should wear a hat or at least ear-muffs in this cold," Brandon admonished, undoubtedly echoing a parental warning. "Mom says it's like a chimney or something."

"Or something," said Luke." Your mom is absolutely right, too." He stopped and reached into his coat to pull out his wallet. He removed two twenty-dollar bills and gave one to each boy.

They stared at the bills, stupefied by the amount. So was Brenna. The two dollars apiece she usually slipped them seemed incredibly paltry compared to Luke's largess.

"Thanks for taking care of Brenna's place, guys," Luke boomed.

He led Brenna to the porch, shielding her from the wind as she fumbled with her key in the lock.

"Can I come in?" he asked quietly, as she pushed open the door. "For a cup of coffee?"

Brenna went still and gulped for breath.

"Wait, I just remembered, you don't have any coffee because you don't like it." Luke leaned his arm against the doorjamb, watching her. "Okay, I'll go with hot chocolate, then. I've been known to choke down tea at times, too."

Brenna reminded herself that it was midmorning, that he had driven her to and from the courthouse in this inclement weather, inconveniencing himself. Plus, the road to his house was currently inaccessible.

The least she could do was to provide him with a hot drink before sending him on his way—wherever that may be.

"How about it, Brenna?" His voice was so soft, she had to lean closer to him to hear it.

Their eyes met again, and she knew that if she were to invite him inside this morning, it would be for more than a hot drink. As for sending him on his way...

"Come in, Luke," she heard herself say.

They entered the house, and he closed the door behind him. With the snow covering the windows and blocking the sight of the outdoors, it seemed as if they were the only two people in the world.

Brenna stood, tense and expectant and aching. She had just given her okay to recreate the sensual events of last night, hadn't she?

Her heartbeat pounded in her ears, her breathing was shaky and shallow. She waited for Luke to make his move and wondered how she would react to him this time....

Six

"**I**'ll put on water for the hot chocolate," Luke called over his shoulder as he strode toward the kitchen. "Do you have anything to eat? I skipped breakfast and I'm starving."

Brenna stood in the foyer, nonplussed. She'd expected him to make a move, but on her, not her kitchen. She heard him turn on the faucet to fill her kettle with water; she listened as the refrigerator was opened and closed, along with cabinets and drawers.

She walked to the door of the kitchen and peered in to see Luke assembling an assortment of food on the kitchen counter.

"You have everything needed to make one of my specialties." He must have heard her approach because he didn't turn around, remaining busily immersed in his project. "Peanut butter and banana with cream cheese and jelly on honey wheat toast. Care to try it?"

Brenna shuddered. "Never."

"It's nutritious for the baby. Contains all the major food groups. Protein, fruit, dairy, grains."

"Thanks, but the baby and I will pass. I have some chicken left over from dinner last night." She entered the kitchen, moving toward the counter where Luke stood. "Wouldn't you rather make a sandwich with chicken?"

"No, but I'll make one for you if you want."

She shook her head. "I'm not hungry for lunch yet. "

She eyed him dubiously as he spread a third slice of bread with cream cheese. The other two were thick with peanut butter and strawberry jelly. And then he began to chop up the banana. "Are you really going to eat that?"

"Sure. It's one of my all time faves. I'm not much of a cook, but I'm a helluva sandwich maker. You could say I'm a professional one, from all the years I put in as sandwich boy in the family tavern kitchen."

Brenna moved a step closer. "Your family owns a tavern?"

"The eponymous Minteer's Tavern in Johnstown. It's been run by Minteers since before the famous flood swept it away. The family rebuilt, and it's been open and operating six days a week from noon to 2:00 a.m., staffed mainly by Minteers."

"Your roots in this area go way back." She came to stand beside him, watching him build his revolting concoction. "No wonder you wanted to come back here, no matter what."

"I'm touched that you would attribute such noble motives to me. Which poses something of a dilemma. Should I play along or tell you the truth about my return?" Luke mused lightly.

"Last call. Are you sure you don't want one?" He put the finishing touches on his sandwich and carried it over to the table.

"Believe me, I'm sure." The kettle began to whistle.

Brenna removed it from the burner and began to prepare two cups of hot chocolate. "But I am curious why you came back here when your family was so furious with you. I've been wondering about that since I first heard it."

"Wonder no more, Brenna. I came back because after Matt fired me, I was as furious with the family as they were with me. And I knew *nothing* would enrage them more than having me living here in the area, when they couldn't stand the sight of me."

He took a hearty bite of his sandwich, reaching over to pull out a chair for Brenna as she carried the steaming mugs to the table.

"Coming back home was the best revenge I could think of. The success of my book was the frosting on the cake, so to speak," he added, grinning.

Brenna sipped her chocolate. "I don't know if I believe you."

"Well, I didn't have to come back here, I had other choices. My services as a political operative were in big demand—outside Matt's district, that is. I had plenty of contacts, and it was well-known that I knew how to play the game of politics."

"But you'd condoned dirty tricks and things," Brenna reminded him. "You had a bad reputation."

"Honey, in some circles those were considered the outstanding features on my résumé. But moving to some other state—especially a faraway one like California where my most tempting offer came from—would've been exactly what my family wanted. Me, the black sheep, out of sight and out of mind. I was too mad at Matt, at my folks, at everybody, to be so accommodating."

"So instead of conveniently disappearing, you came back and worked on your grisly crime book—and it turned out to be a big success."

"Meanwhile, I showed up everywhere, at church, at the

tavern, at every family member's birthday or baptism or funeral. My very presence was an affront, and I relished every moment.''

Brenna wasn't sure if she bought his perverse motive for his return or not. She suspected the true reasons were a lot more complex than Luke allowed himself to believe. ''Are you still so angry with all of them?''

''No, not anymore. After all, things worked out pretty well. If I hadn't come back, I wouldn't have written the book and found a whole new career. Turns out that I like writing more than politics—not to mention that it pays better if you happen to hit the bestseller jackpot.''

''What about your family?'' Brenna watched him finish his sandwich, down to the last crumb. ''Are they still mad at you?''

''A bunch of them still disapprove of me, but I think they're mellowing. They've finally resigned themselves to seeing me around the district. When my house was finished, I threw a big housewarming party and everybody came. Mainly to tell me I was nuts to build a place on the mountain so far from town.''

''With weather like this, they have a point,'' observed Brenna, as a heavy blob of snow dropped from the kitchen window.

''Nah, I knew exactly what I was doing when I bought my lot dirt cheap a couple years ago. Several new houses are being built out there. It's a great place to live, and word is getting out, increasing property values. There's a fantastic view, big lots, plenty of privacy and—''

''You sound like a real estate agent trying to close a sale,'' Brenna interjected dryly. ''Naturally, that pesky, road-inaccessibility factor isn't mentioned.''

''Downed trees and power lines are freak accidents,'' protested Luke. ''And the road will be open by tonight, if I'm lucky.''

He glanced at his watch. "Well, I'd better get going. I'm sure you have stuff to do, and my laptop is in the car, so I'll head to the library to work on my book. Thanks for the late breakfast—or early lunch. I guess we'll have to call it brunch," he concluded.

He rose from his chair.

Brenna gaped at him. "You're leaving?"

Disappointment tore through her, and though she quickly lowered her head, she had a sinking feeling he had seen it in her eyes, on her face, in those first unguarded seconds.

"That surprises you?" Luke stood over her. "Why?"

When Brenna lifted her head to meet his penetrating blue eyes, her impassive mask was firmly in place.

"I'd better stop wasting time and get upstairs to work if I want to finish my paper-doll book before the baby is born. I've been contracted to do a series called Children of the Twentieth Century, decade by decade, and I'm only in the first one. The ohs or the aughts. Who knows what to call it? It's the same dilemma we're having in this century."

"You're babbling," Luke said bluntly. "I'd like an answer to my question."

"I'd forgotten that talking about my work bores you." Brenna tried a diversionary tactic. "Don't worry, I won't do it again."

Her tactic didn't work; Luke was not diverted. "You expected me to try a repeat of last night, didn't you?"

Brenna winced. "I know you're busy and have work to do. So do I. I completely understand."

To her horror her voice trembled and she felt sudden, unexpected tears welling in her eyes. What a rotten time for her hormones to run amok! Brenna swallowed hard, pressing her lips together tightly, fighting for control. Not for anything would she let her hormones make her cry.

"Exactly what do you *think* you understand, Brenna?" Luke's tone was almost mocking.

"Just drop it, okay?" snapped Brenna. "Believe me, I'm well aware that I'm almost nine months pregnant and as big as a...a cow. I don't blame you at all for wanting to leave."

Immediately, she clapped her hands over her mouth in dismay. "I didn't mean to say that! It—the words just slipped out. Oh, I really am acting like a hormonal head-case—just like your aunt Molly!"

"Compared to Aunt Molly's antics, you're as repressed and restrained as a Puritan, Brenna. And you're not big as a cow, and I'm not leaving because I don't want to stay with you."

"Yes, of course, you have a deadline to meet," she murmured, striving to regain her lost poise. And to once more offer him the diplomatic out.

Which Luke immediately rejected. "My deadline isn't a problem. I have plenty of time before my book is due."

"I see," Brenna said tautly.

"No, you don't see," growled Luke. "I'm leaving because if I stay, I'll give in to the need to touch you, I'll pull you into my arms and kiss you until you're moaning and sighing and clinging to me the way you did last night. And then I'll pick you up and carry you upstairs...and scare the hell out of you, the way I did last night."

He laid his hand on the top of her head, smoothing his fingers over her silky dark hair. "I'm not a Neanderthal, remember? I'm not going to go caveman on a woman who was raped and is still traumatized by—"

Brenna jumped to her feet, nearly knocking over her mug and her chair in the process. "How did you know I was raped? Who told you? Who else knows? I didn't tell anybody in this area, I haven't told anyone in years."

"Nobody told me, Brenna. And if you haven't told anyone around here, I'm sure nobody knows. But I had enough clues to put it together." He cleared his throat. "You don't want to talk about it, I know. That much you've told me."

"It's not a place in the past I care to return to," she said bitterly. "Talking about it takes me there."

"Return to?" Luke slowly rubbed his hand along the length of her arm. "Sweetheart, I don't think you've ever left it. You're still stuck there. Your trip to the sperm bank, your determination to avoid a relationship with a man, the way you flipped out last night when it looked like we were going to have sex—it all adds up to some serious, er, issues, Brenna."

"I think I'm coping very well!"

"Yes, yes, you are," Luke agreed quickly, his tone tender and supportive. "And I'm not going to do anything to, uh, take away from how well you're coping. Or give you more to cope with." He looked tense and increasingly flustered. "I can't exactly find the right words, but do you get what I'm trying to say?"

She nodded her head. "Yes."

And she did; she understood what he was trying to say to her on every level.

Brenna felt her apprehensive reserve dissolving fast and wondered how Luke inspired such confidence within her. Why was she able to drop her guard—the impenetrable one she'd maintained for years—only with him?

He was a renegade and a rogue but had been honest and open about it. And early on, she had gleaned that there were good qualities within his character, at odds with his purported reputation. From his treatment of her, she knew she'd been right.

"I get it, Luke."

"Good!" Luke sounded relieved. "I've never been so inarticulate before. I can usually make my point at least, though I've never been known for making it with eloquence."

"And eloquence is a prized commodity in politics, isn't it?" The corners of her lips slowly curved into a smile. "Especially when it's packed into a twenty-second sound bite."

"True. Luckily, I was never a speechwriter. I can play a good game behind the scenes, but when it comes to talking the talk... That's my brother Matt's department, and he excels in it."

He leaned down and kissed her forehead. "Getting back on topic—I wish I could find some eloquent way to say I'm sorry you were so badly hurt, Brenna."

"You are eloquent. Because I know you mean it, Luke." To his obvious surprise, she linked her arms around his neck. "I don't want to be stuck in the past. And when I'm with you, for the first time ever, I feel different. I feel brave."

"I'm glad, Brenna."

"It's more than that." She gulped. "To be perfectly honest, you make me feel things I didn't know I could ever feel. And I was scared last night, at first, but then, later..." Her voice trailed off.

"Then, later, you decided that maybe you weren't so scared?" He rubbed his nose lightly, affectionately, against hers.

"When you came in the house with me today—" she moved closer to him, her eyes closing as he continued to gently nuzzle her "—I thought that maybe, if something happened this time, I might, I could—well, I didn't think I would flip out," she added wryly, using his own description of her reaction.

"Maybe if something happened?" challenged Luke. "Come on, Brenna, take it a step further and admit that you *expected* something to happen when you invited me in today. You *wanted* it to happen. You still do."

"And if I don't admit it, you'll probably tell me in exact detail how you've drawn that conclusion?"

"Baby, there's no *probably* about it, I'll *definitely* tell you. You looked crushed when I said I was leaving, you looked like you were ready to burst into tears."

She opened her mouth to automatically, defensively, deny it. And ended up balling her fingers into a fist and lightly punching his arm.

"Jerk," she muttered, not without a certain affection.

"Thank you, darling." His hand enclosed her fist and carried it to his mouth. He kissed her knuckles. "That's one of the nicer terms used to describe me."

They both ended up laughing. Brenna was amazed. What could've turned into a dreadful, melodramatic scene had ended in laughter.

She looked into his warm-blue eyes and knew then and there that she loved him. It had happened impossibly, ridiculously fast, but the real miracle was that it had happened at all.

She had given up any hope of falling in love years ago, believing she was too damaged by the sexual trauma in her past to overcome it. But it seemed that she had, because she knew she was in love with Luke Minteer...and she wanted desperately to make love with him.

"Show me where you work," Luke said, cupping the nape of her neck with his hand. He headed in the direction of the staircase, taking her along with him. "In case a translation is needed, I'm encouraging you to invite me up to see your etchings."

"Consider yourself invited. But we'll walk up the stairs this time. I don't want you to break your back trying to carry me."

"I could smoothly counter that you're not heavy, you're a mere featherweight, except you'd probably punch me and call me a jerk again," said Luke, taking her hand in his.

"Hey, there's no *probably* about it, I'll *definitely* tell you."

They mounted the staircase, holding hands.

Her studio was at the top of the stairs, her bedroom two doors down the narrow hallway. Brenna hesitated for a moment.

And then Luke dropped her hand and strode swiftly into her studio, directly to her draft table.

"Hey, this is really good!" He stared at the completed full-color drawing of Kristin, which Brenna had finished the night before.

"The little girl looks like a real kid. Everything you've drawn looks real—the baby doll, the clothes, the kitten. As for the title of the book, here is a little professional advice—you should label the first decade of the century The Ohs. *Aught* sounds like a joke."

"Is that advice from your experience in politics or publishing?" Her voice wavered.

"Both. *Aught* just doesn't work." Luke looked up at Brenna, who was still standing in the hall. "Show me some more stuff you've done, Brenna. I want to see all of it."

She stared at him, confused and uncertain. Hadn't they come upstairs to…go into her bedroom?

Luke had no trouble deciphering the silent question in her eyes.

"I'm not going to pounce on you, Brenna. Show me your work, tell me about it."

He glanced outside. "From the way this snow is coming down, we aren't going anywhere anytime soon. We have all the time in the world. I'm not going to rush things. Okay?"

"I'll cede to your greater experience in this area," Brenna said, surprising herself with the small joke. She never joked about anything remotely sexual.

"Good. Now come in here…"

Brenna enjoyed showing Luke her work, the greeting cards and sewing patterns, the paper-doll books, the artwork she'd done for various children's books and magazines over the past few years.

She kept one copy of everything she'd had published in a bookcase, and Luke picked up each item and studied it with interest.

Brenna was flattered by the attention; she couldn't deny it.

The number of paper-doll books that she had researched and drawn visibly astounded Luke. There was the set of Century Women's Wear, a series of ten books covering various women's fashions over the past millennium. The Century Children Series, including ten books featuring children and their clothing and playthings of the past millennium. The Children of the World series, featuring ten books filled with children from each continent and their ethnic costumes and toys.

"You've done *thirty* of these paper-doll books—plus all these other things!" Luke exclaimed, impressed. "And each paper-doll book has sixteen pages of drawings—I counted them! How do you do it, Brenna? You're too young to have been working for very many years. Unless you started when you were about four?"

Brenna smiled. "I started drawing about then, but I published my first book when I was in art school."

"At The Rocky Mountain College of Art and Design in Denver," interjected Luke. "I read your bio sketch in one of your books here. Is speed-drawing a course requirement there?"

He was now leafing through the several dozen children's magazines, each featuring a paper-doll or paper-toy page by Brenna Morgan.

"I work fast, and I work all the time." Brenna gave the

same answer she always did when asked about her prolific talent.

She didn't feel it necessary to mention that chronic insomnia added many hours to her working day. She didn't go to bed until she was so exhausted she literally fell asleep the moment her head hit the pillow.

"Hmm, that sounds like a stock answer," Luke observed. "I can spot them instantly, they're a prerequisite in politics. I also have a few of my own for writing, especially when I'm asked where I get my ideas."

"Do you say you subscribe to *The Serial Killer's Digest?*"

"How did you know? Although, I actually say *Murderers' Monthly* or *The Gruesome Gazette*. But I like your little jest better. Mind if I swipe it?"

"Be my guest."

"How many of your paper-doll books are still in print?" He studied an *Asian Children of the World* book with all the elaborate paper-doll costumes she had drawn and colored.

"All of them. The publishers said they have no plans to discontinue any of them," she added modestly.

Luke gaped at her. "I'm no authority on publishing, but I know that means all your books must be selling well. And you have a contract for a new series, too. You've got to be some kind of publishing phenom, Brenna!"

She shrugged. "I'm just grateful I'm able to earn a living doing what I enjoy. And that I'll be able to support my baby. My publishers were kind of depressed when I told them about the baby, because I also said that I intend to slow down considerably."

"The baby," Luke murmured. He gazed down at her pregnant belly, bulging beneath her dark-rose maternity tunic top. "Sometimes when we're talking, I actually forget you're pregnant."

"Hmm, have you had your eyes checked lately?" She chuckled. "There could be some problem with your sight. My pregnancy is the most noticeable thing about me these days."

"It was the first thing I noticed about you when we met. But not too long afterward, I stopped giving your figure— or the lack of it—a thought." He smiled sheepishly. "I have to admit that's a first for me."

"I'm guessing that you've always required a shapely woman on your arm?" Brenna dared to tease.

"Oh, yeah. And other places, too." Luke's eyes gleamed. "Go on and call me a shallow jerk."

"Only if you'll call me a frigid headcase."

Moving slowly, as if not to startle her, Luke wrapped his arms around her in an embrace that was more protective than amorous. "It's not the same at all. Shallow jerks make choices, but you didn't have a choice, Brenna. You were struck by circumstances beyond your control."

"You've never even heard the details, and you're giving me the benefit of the doubt?" Brenna leaned against him, letting her head loll against the hard wall of his chest. "That means a lot to me, Luke. And I really don't think you're a shallow jerk—although maybe you used to be one," she couldn't help but add, looking up at him, her gaze unmistakably flirtatious.

Luke's response was immediate. He scooped her up in his arms, grinning as she gave a surprised squeak.

"Luke, I can walk!"

"I know. But I want you to trust me enough to let me carry you."

"This is supposed to be a love scene, isn't it? Not an…an Outward Bound experiment in building trust."

Luke laughed. "Maybe it's both. Do you trust me not to drop you *and* to make love with you?"

Brenna considered it. "I must. Because here we are."

"Yeah, here we are."

He claimed a fiery kiss before he carried her from her studio into her bedroom, holding her high against his chest. Brenna relaxed against him, her lips brushing along his jawline. Daringly she allowed the tip of her tongue to taste his salty skin.

Inside her bedroom Luke set her gently on her feet, facing him. He framed her face with his hands, kissing her forehead, the tip of her nose, the curve of each high cheekbone.

By the time he finally claimed her mouth, she was shivering with anticipation.

Her lips opened on impact, admitting his tongue inside. It seemed perfectly natural to welcome him by rubbing her tongue softly against his.

Brenna heard his moan and enjoyed the rush of sensual feminine power that filled her.

They stood together kissing, one long, deep kiss melding into another. Their kisses were both leisurely and urgent, ravenous but fulfilling, an exciting sensual paradox.

"Who'd have ever thought kissing could be this good?" Luke wondered aloud.

Both were panting and breathless when they finally had to surface for air.

"You sound downright awestruck." Brenna touched her fingers to her lips that were moist and swollen from his kisses, then traced his own mouth, equally moist and swollen from kissing her.

"I am. Once I, er, reached a certain age and a certain stage, I viewed kissing as a strictly preliminary step, to be gotten through as quickly as possible to reach the main event. But with you—" his expression was one of almost comical astonishment "—it's like kissing *is* the main event."

Brenna smiled. "That's very romantic, I think."

"Come here."

Luke turned her around and pulled her back against him, fitting her into the hard male frame of his body. He moved his big hands along the length of her arms, then back to her shoulders. Pushing aside her hair with his fingers, he kissed the curve of her neck, nibbling with his teeth, soothing the sensitized skin with his tongue.

And then he slid one hand down her back, following the zipper of her maternity tunic top.

"Let me take it off," he whispered huskily, his nimble fingers already unzipping.

Brenna drew a quick breath. If she didn't want this to proceed any further, now was the time to speak up.

But she didn't say a word as he peeled the unzipped tunic open and slowly moved it down her arms, over her breasts, over her bulging belly. It finally landed in a deep rose-colored pool at her feet.

Brenna stared down at her breasts, cupped firmly in her well-fitted maternity bra, designed for exactly that purpose. She laid one hand on the stretch panel of her maternity leggings that covered the hard swell of her abdomen. Within her womb, the baby was quiet, probably sleeping. There was no movement to observe beneath the material.

"Like we said earlier, this…this shape isn't what you're used to seeing when you're in a woman's bedroom," she said faintly.

"No, it isn't," Luke agreed.

For a moment she imagined the women in his past, those women whose curvaceous figures had tantalized him. But the past was just that, past. And if he was no longer a shallow jerk who demanded certain things, then she wasn't a frigid headcase to be intimidated by them.

Luke linked his hand with her own, interlacing their fingers. His other hand covered hers, which rested on her belly.

"I like the way you look, Brenna." His voice was husky.

She glowed from the warmth in his tone. It mingled with a raw sensuality that enticed, rather than unnerved her. She couldn't resist him or these wonderful feelings he was evoking within her.

An urgent need to feel his lips on hers again surged through her, and she turned in his arms, clasping his head with her hands to kiss him until she felt too dizzy to stand. But there was no cause for concern, for standing was no longer required.

Luke picked her up again and carried her over to her bed. With precision expertise, he pulled off the flowered quilt comforter while still holding her, then carefully placed her in the center of the bed, on the matching flowered sheets.

Standing beside the bed, he deftly, swiftly, pulled off his clothes.

Brenna stared at him, her eyes wide. He was muscled and well built, his body fully aroused and taut with desire. A thin sheen of sweat glistened on his skin. The sight literally took her breath away.

Luke noticed. "Breathe, Brenna," he reminded her, and reached out his hand to smooth her hair. "Are you sure you're okay with this? Because you don't have to. You know that, don't you?"

He waited for her answer.

His control, his concern for her, despite his own heightened state of desire, reassured her.

Brenna met his blue eyes, which glittered with sexual hunger. He wanted her, but he wouldn't force her if she were to call things to a halt right now.

Which she didn't want to do, Brenna realized with certainty.

She wanted this; she wanted him…because she loved him. Brenna put her hand on Luke's.

He responded at once to her invitation and sat down beside her on the bed.

"I know I don't *have* to," she murmured. "It's my choice." Just saying the words empowered her.

"And you choose me," he said huskily. "I'm glad, Brenna. And proud, too. I'm proud of you." He gazed at her. "I admire your courage and your resolve in handling whatever was thrown your way."

His eyes, his tone, his expression, invited her to confide in him, to tell him about whatever had been thrown her way.

Brenna shifted. "Luke, I don't want to tell you my life story, especially not here. And especially not now. I just want this to be between you and me, with no ghosts from the past."

"Okay. But can I say that from what I've guessed, you were dealt a crummy hand and played it well? And that having a woman like you want me, only me—well, it validates me. Do you get what I'm trying to say, Brenna?"

"I hope it's not that you see me as some kind of ticket to redemption for your, uh, disreputable past?" she asked lightly. "Because that is one melodramatic role I don't care to play."

"I see you as a woman I want very much." He smiled into her eyes. "Better?"

"Much."

Luke unhooked the back clasp of her maternity bra and slowly drew it from her body. Her breasts were swollen and full. He liked the idea that nature—not silicone implants—was responsible for the enhancement.

He continued to stare. Her nipples were large, dark and taut. The size of her nipples fascinated him; they were full and pouty, ready to nurse a child. He had never seen the breasts of a pregnant woman before and had never wanted to, but the sight of Brenna transfixed him.

Their mouths met in another slow, sultry kiss while one of his hands moved lightly over her breasts, cupping one, then the other, learning the feel and shape of each. His fingers caressed her nipples, circling the aureoles, toying with the full, tight tips.

Brenna whimpered, twisting closer, clinging to him. It was so much, so pleasurable and exciting, yet she needed, she wanted…more.

As if magically attuned to her thoughts, Luke proceeded to undress her. There was a time when she would have been mortified to be naked in front of any man—and to be naked and pregnant in a male's presence would've been awful beyond imagining.

But being here, doing this with Luke, felt neither embarrassing or unreal.

It felt good. It felt as if this was the way it was supposed to be.

They lay down on the bed together, nude, their bodies entwined, kissing and caressing for an endless time. Brenna felt his manhood, hot and swollen pressing against her, and curiosity and desire flooded her, drowning her past fears in a tidal wave of passion.

She was on the verge of reaching for him, of succumbing to the unexpected need of touching him *there,* when he lifted his lips from hers and glided his hands over her belly, over her hips.

"I can't get enough of you, Brenna," he whispered, nibbling on her neck. "The more I touch you, the more I taste you, it's not enough."

His words swirled through her head as he kissed her along the length of her collarbone, then moved his mouth lower, to her breasts. He nipped and suckled her, lightly grazing her ultrasensitive skin, teasing each rosy peak.

The sensation was excruciatingly pleasurable, like nothing she had ever known. She wanted him to stop, because she didn't think it was possible to sustain this level of phys-ical intensity, she wanted him to go on and on and never stop....

And then his lips continued a downward path along her body, probing her belly button, which pregnancy had pushed outward, with his tongue, nuzzling her abdomen. And moved lower...

Brenna gasped for breath when it dawned on her where he was heading, what he was intent on doing with his mouth....

She grabbed a fistful of his hair, abruptly stopping him.

Luke raised his head and looked at her, his blue eyes questioning.

"Sorry. I...didn't mean to pull your hair out by the roots." She released her grip and sat up. "But I—I've never—" she blurted out, blushing. She turned her head, unable to hold his gaze. "Luke, I've never done that before. I—I've never even tried the...the, uh, missionary posi-tion."

She cringed, blushing fiercely. "What I'm trying to say is that I'm not experienced at sex."

With violence, yes. She had experienced that. The ad-dendum leaped into her head, but she didn't say it aloud and she pushed the thought away. No ghosts from the past allowed, not here and not now.

"I pretty much figured your sexual experience was lim-ited," Luke said conversationally, pulling himself up to sit beside her. "And if you wouldn't even try the venerable old missionary position—conservative enough, even for missionaries!—of course you would never attempt anything else. You especially wouldn't allow an intimacy that means giving up total control, opening yourself completely both emotionally and physically—"

"You sound like a sex therapist on cable!" Brenna in-terjected hotly.

"If that's a compliment, thanks. If it's an insult, ouch." Luke shrugged. "But what I mean to say is that I understand, Brenna. There is a lust-into-trust coalition that has to occur, and until it does, you're not ready."

The affection in his tone bolstered her like a shot of brandy. "Does the coalition ever go the other way? From trust into lust?"

"I don't see why it couldn't."

He kissed her long and lingeringly, his hands resuming the gentle fondling of her breasts. Brenna felt herself melting—all her inhibitions, her anxiety and fear, seemed to just flow away.

When their lips briefly parted, they both opened their eyes, and their gazes met and held.

"I don't know which coalition occurred, but I'm ready," she whispered.

She knew she trusted Luke…she certainly lusted for him! She had already granted him intimacies she would never have anticipated with any other man. And she was ready for more.

Luke kissed her again, slowly, taking his time with her, not shortchanging an inch of her skin with his lips as he resumed his intimate journey of her body.

He kissed her legs from her thighs to her ankles, first one and then the other, before parting them with his hands. His mouth nipped and laved the soft skin of her inner thighs, before moving to her center, opening her to him, tasting her.

The intimate contact made her arch instinctively and cry out. She was unprepared for this, after all, and a self-conscious flush suffused her skin from head to toe.

Luke lifted his head and reached for her hand, holding it until she opened her eyes. Brenna saw him watching her, saw the desire in his hot blue gaze.

"Relax, Brenna. Let me take you there." His voice was softly compelling.

"I feel like a freak," she confessed nervously. "Most women my age aren't so...so—"

"You're not a freak, and this is just between the two of us, remember? Other women your age aren't allowed in here."

The warmth and humor, the soothing patience in his tone, convinced her. Brenna's eyelids fluttered shut, and she breathed deeply.

When Luke continued his tender seduction, she gave in to the all-consuming need. And she gave complete control to Luke Minteer.

Complete control.

It was a dizzying surrender. She felt the sensual, primal waves rising and surging within her. Brenna moaned, unable to stay silent as she was swept away in a tornado of whirling emotion, of searing passion and pleasure that built and built until she was sure she would implode from the sheer intensity of it all.

She screamed Luke's name as she shattered into rapturous spasms. A shower of tiny fireworks flashed behind her closed eyes; her whole body pulsed with currents of sensuous electricity.

Slowly, very slowly, she began to drift down from the soaring heights to which he had taken her. His strong arms surrounded her, her head was resting against his chest, his voice low and smooth.

"Luke," she managed to whisper, but her eyelids were so heavy she couldn't lift them.

"I'm here, my love."

Brenna wanted to open her eyes and gaze into Luke's, to tell him about the emotions he had released in her, to thank him for setting her free. For she felt free and light as air, floating in a bubble of pure euphoria.

She wanted to reciprocate, to send him to the same thrilling peaks of ecstasy where he had so unselfishly taken her. But her sated body's demand for sleep overruled her.

Snuggling deeper in his arms, inhaling his unique Luke-scent, Brenna slipped into a deep sleep.

Luke held her, watching her. Her breathing was deep and even, her body totally relaxed. From the pleasure and satisfaction he had given her.

A smile curved his lips. He had given her much pleasure. And though his own body was aching with unassuaged need, he found his lack of fulfillment relatively easy to ignore.

Because the unfamiliar feeling of tenderness that suffused him was something of a reward in itself. Amazingly, by putting her needs first, he had never felt more of a man.

He felt a slight jab on his wrist and looked at her naked belly. Was that a tiny foot or a hand moving under there, making contact with him?

"Are you doing push-ups in there, squirt? Or pretending to kick a soccer ball around?"

He placed his palm over her abdomen and felt the now-rolling movements of the baby within, who had obviously awakened and was exercising.

"Sam or Susie? Which one are you?" He rubbed her tummy as if he were tousling the hair of the child within. "Boy or girl, you're gonna be cute, because your mom is a real babe, if you'll pardon the unpolitically correct expression. And you've also got those tall, blond chromosomes from, uh, the Swedish guy."

For some reason, he couldn't bring himself to refer to the medical student sperm donor as a father. This baby belonged to Brenna; Dr. Test Tube was out of the picture forever.

Which left an opening in her life and in the baby's life,

too. There really ought to be a man in the picture, a man who cared about Brenna and her child.

Luke reached down and grabbed the quilt comforter from the floor, pulling it over Brenna and himself.

Gradually, his body stopped throbbing from unfulfilled urgency, and his arousal faded and dissolved into exhaustion. He fell asleep in Brenna's bed, his arms protectively cradling her and the unborn baby.

Seven

Brenna awakened, feeling groggy and disoriented.

She glanced around her bedroom and noticed that the curtains weren't drawn. For her to be in bed with the curtains open was a definite anomaly; she ritually closed them before climbing into bed at night.

Focusing more clearly, she saw snowflakes falling desultorily outside the window and realized that it wasn't nighttime, after all. The skies were gray and cloudy, but it was definitely daylight out there.

And then, abruptly, Brenna came fully awake and sat upright in bed, as if struck by a bolt of lightning.

She was nude under her quilt! The sensual memories accompanying that observation struck her with avalanche force.

Brenna sprang from the bed as fast as her pregnant shape would permit, ignoring her clothes, which were still on the floor where Luke had dropped them while undressing her.

She snatched her oversize fleecy blue robe and pulled it on, shivering, though she felt hot, as if her entire body was one heated red blush.

Perhaps she woke the baby with her fast and frantic motions, because all at once she felt him/her turning a somersault, first one way, then the other.

And while the baby enjoyed its afternoon workout, Brenna thought of herself with Luke, visualizing him, feeling the touch of his lips…

What had she done?

Oh, what she had done!

"I'm sorry," she whispered aloud, her hand on her belly.

The words echoed in her head, mocking her. How many times had she heard *I'm sorry* from her mother after Marly had done something extraordinarily stupid? Enough times to discount the apology completely and to know that there would be another one, equally meaningless, forthcoming after Marly's next misadventure.

And now here she was, Brenna herself, repeating the same words to her own child after having a misadventure of her own.

That it was a misadventure, Brenna had no doubt. The fact that she was alone, that Luke Minteer was gone, spoke volumes. Marly Morgan inevitably had ended up alone, too. Brenna groaned aloud.

She should head right into her studio and get to work putting the final polishing touches on Kristin's wardrobe. She could lose herself in that world, in the decade of the "ohs."

Not *aught*.

Once again Luke filled her head.

Brenna headed purposefully into the bathroom, turned on the shower and shed her robe. The warm water sluiced over her skin, and she rubbed coconut-scented liquid soap over her body.

She willed herself not think about her mother or about Luke Minteer. Somehow, here in the shower, it was easier to occupy her mind with other things. Like her work.

Since she was almost done with the Kristin paper doll, she would concentrate on the next decade of the twentieth century, the teens. At least she knew what to dub that decade. World War I had dominated the teens, so she would draw a little boy with toy soldiers and flags and a hat made from folded newspapers. He would have a hobby horse and a puppy....

Brenna was deciding what to name her paper-doll boy—Simon, perhaps?—as she climbed out of the shower and wrapped a big beach towel around her. She'd bought several to use after showering as her pregnancy advanced.

She was lost in thought, picturing little Simon in the early months of 1918, deciding which books would best serve as references for that particular period.

The last thing she expected was to find someone in her hallway.

So when she literally walked right into Luke Minteer, Brenna was caught completely off guard.

She let out a bloodcurdling scream.

Luke was so startled by her outburst that he gasped, and they both jumped back, to stand a few paces apart and stare wide-eyed at each other.

Luke recovered first. "I heard water running and knew you were up."

He attempted to smile. It was more than obvious that Brenna was stunned by the sight of him. Alarmed, too?

"What are you doing here?" she asked warily.

"Brenna, why wouldn't I be here?"

She looked genuinely perplexed, and Luke frowned.

"I got up about two hours ago. You were sleeping soundly and I figured you wouldn't wake up for a while, so I went out to my car and got my laptop. I've been working downstairs in the kitchen.''

"Oh.''

"Did you think I'd left?'' Luke's brows narrowed and he studied her intently. "Or are you on some Lady MacBeth guilt trip, taking a shower, attempting to wash away all traces of—''

"Oh, please! I'm not *that* clichéd!''

"It's not a cliché, it's an image. A powerful image. I used it in my first book. The killer's girlfriend washes her hands compulsively after finding out what her lover has been up to.''

Brenna rolled her eyes. "The more I hear about that book, the worse it sounds.''

"Yeah, I'm starting to hate it myself, although I'll always love those royalty checks from it. The new book I'm working on is much better.''

They looked at each other.

"You'd better dry off and get some clothes on,'' Luke said at last. "It's chilly in here. This house is definitely not energy efficient. Your heating bills must make gas company officials smile.''

As he mentioned it, Brenna felt the cool air on her damp skin. Her freshly shampooed hair was under the towel she'd wound around it, turban-style. She was also suddenly aware that while she stood here wearing only a beach towel, Luke was fully dressed.

"The road to your house is blocked. It won't be open until tonight, if then,'' she said carefully.

"That's not the reason why I'm still here, Brenna.'' Luke heaved a sigh. "Although I know convincing you of that isn't going to be easy. You practically jumped out of your skin when you saw me because you were sure I'd taken off. How am I reading you so far? Right on target?''

She nodded her head.

"Will you let me take you to bed and show you I—"

"No!" exclaimed Brenna. "I just want to get dried and dressed."

"Okay, I hear you." Luke shrugged. "I'll be downstairs writing in the kitchen."

He turned and headed down the stairs, leaving a flummoxed Brenna standing in the hall. Luke hadn't left. He wasn't acting any differently toward her despite their intimate interlude earlier.

She hadn't anticipated this turn of events and wasn't sure what they portended. It was mind-bending to have your entire world view altered in an afternoon, and being naked and wet only made it more surreal.

Brenna quickly put on a chocolate-brown maternity outfit with matching shirt and pants and dried her hair.

Next, she went into her studio. She took some notes, bookmarked several pages of her reference books and even did a quick preliminary sketch of Simon. Though immersed in her work, she didn't forget for an instant that Luke Minteer was downstairs in her kitchen, writing about a serial killer.

But she was back in control of herself and worked for almost three hours before allowing herself to venture downstairs. Since she'd heard no doors opening or closing and no car engines starting, she knew Luke hadn't left the house.

And sure enough, there at her kitchen table sat Luke Minteer, working on his laptop, just as he'd said. Even forewarned, the sight amazed her. She paused on the threshold, and Luke looked up.

Their eyes met.

"Yeah, I'm still here," he said dryly. "And you're still shocked that I am. By the way, I heard on the radio that route 128 was opened about a half hour ago, so that reason is eliminated, Brenna."

"They must've sent extra crews to get the work done so fast," she suggested weakly.

"They must've. If I were to say that the reason it was taken care of so quickly is because the mayor's daughter and her family live up there, I'd sound cynical, wouldn't I?"

"Very cynical," she agreed. "I'm sure His Honor is deeply concerned about *all* his constituents being inconvenienced by downed trees and power lines."

Luke laughed and turned in his chair, holding his arms open to her. "Get over here, Brenna."

Acting on pure impulse, without giving herself time to think or consider or analyze, Brenna rushed into his arms. Luke pulled her down on his lap and held her, as she buried her head in the hollow of his shoulder.

"This is how it should've been when you first woke up," he said quietly. "I should've— "

"There was nothing you *should* have done, Luke. Nothing you could have done. I probably would've been just as spooked if you'd been there when I first woke up. And then we probably would've had a fight and I would've kicked you out." She smiled up at him. "At least this way we avoided a scene, and we both got some work done."

"It's been a very productive day." His tone gave the innocuous words a sensual meaning all their own. And then he kissed her gently, lingeringly.

When he lifted his lips, she gave a small, contented sigh and rested against him.

"Brenna, I want you to know that even if we'd had a big fight and you'd kicked me out, I would still be here. And not because of the snow or the road."

"Because when ordered to leave, you take it as a challenge and deliberately stay put. Irritates the hell out of people." She repeated his boast back to him, softly brushing her lips over his as she spoke.

"True. But in your case, my motives are worthier. I'm here because I want to be with you, Brenna."

They kissed, tenderly at first, then deeply, torridly, with a burning urgency. Luke resisted the almost overwhelming desire to take her back to bed, to seek the satisfaction he had so unselfishly denied himself earlier.

Brenna gave no signs of being averse to that; it would be the natural progression of such fierce, ardent passion.

And yet, instead of doing what he wanted, Luke found himself in the unique position of being unselfish yet again.

"You haven't eaten since breakfast," he heard himself say.

He was putting his sexual urges on hold and her nutritional needs first? Now that was a new one. Plus, he sounded a lot like Grandmother Minteer. She faithfully kept track of who'd eaten what and when while under the same roof.

"You and the baby need some food," he added, sounding even more Grandmotheresque.

Brenna laid her hands on his shoulders. "I don't feel hungry for food right now," she murmured, her dark eyes cloudy with desire.

"Sam or Susie begs to differ." Luke's hand rested on his abdomen and felt the wild dance going on within her womb. "He or she is going to kick its way out of there if you don't send down some chow right away."

As if to second Luke's observation, her stomach growled, an embarrassingly loud noise that could not be ignored.

"I guess you're right." Blushing, Brenna stood up. "I'll make spaghetti. I have marinara sauce and meatballs from Volario's Market. Would you like to stay for dinner?" she added uncertainly.

Luke gazed at her kiss-swollen lips and her tousled hair

and decided he'd never seen such an erotic picture. "Oh, yeah. I'd like to stay."

After they'd eaten, they sat at the table and talked. Luke told her a bit about the new direction his novel was taking; she told him about her plans for little Simon and his World War I era toys and clothes.

"Calling a paper doll Simon is a good way to get that name out of your system," Luke approved. "So now if the baby's a boy, you'll name him Sam?"

"Your campaign against Simon has been surprisingly effective," acknowledged Brenna. "I've decided against using it. But Sam is a name that comes with its own baggage. Uncle Sam, Yosemite Sam, Son of Sam. No, I'm not going with Sam, either. I think I'll switch to another letter of the alphabet."

"How about *X?* I think Xerxes has a certain ring to it."

"It has the ring of getting beat up in the schoolyard."

"Okay, let's try *L.* What about Lucas? It has all the masculine charm, strength and popularity of Luke but is slightly different. And you could add Minteer, too. Around here the name Minteer is golden."

"Don't you think the name Lucas Minteer Morgan might cause some talk around town?"

"So what?" Luke grinned. "Talk is cheap. And today's big news is tomorrow's nobody-gives-a-damn-about-it story. A whole industry is based on that infallible premise—it's called publicity, and a savvy PR person can—"

"You might be right, but I've been the subject of enough gossip to last a lifetime," Brenna cut in fervently. "I don't want to be big news for even one day. Now that I'm here where nobody knows anything about me, I intend to stay blissfully anonymous."

Luke's mood, his expression, abruptly shifted from light-hearted to dark.

"Don't," Brenna whispered.

"Don't what?"

"Don't look that way. So angry, so filled with hostility."

"But that's how I feel when I think about you being hurt. I'd like to dismember the creep who did it, and I don't need any of the details, Brenna. It's enough to know that you were raped by some scumbag, and if I could kill the guy—"

"You can't. Someone beat you to it."

The odd expression on her face, the way her voice trembled, told him that the "someone" was not irrelevant to the case. Or to Brenna.

"Will you tell me who did?" he asked quietly.

"My mother." She lifted her chin and met his eyes. "He was her latest boyfriend. I told her right after he moved in—Mom's boyfriends inevitably moved in with us or we moved in with them, after they'd been dating a week or two—that the way he acted around me was scary. She laughed it off and told me I was being prissy, that he was just a fun-loving teaser. No big deal, she said."

"God, Brenna." Luke laid his hand over hers and she grasped it, wrapping her fingers tightly around his.

"Turned out she was wrong. One night when Mom went out with some friends from work, he came into my room and raped me," she said flatly.

Luke muttered an expletive.

Brenna swallowed hard and then determinedly pasted a practiced smile on her face. "But that was a long time ago, thirteen years ago, another lifetime ago, for all practical purposes. I don't dwell on it, I've moved on with my life."

Luke knew she was giving him the chance to drop the charged topic and switch to something less sordid. To something superficial and pleasant. He also knew there was a time when he would've eagerly done just that. He had never been one to willingly open himself to another's pain.

But today he didn't try to escape hearing about the pain

and horror Brenna had faced. It was a part of her, and he realized that he wanted *all* of her. Not just the pleasant social side she showed everybody else, but everything that she was.

"Thirteen years ago, you were only thirteen! Brenna, you were just a little girl!"

Luke felt rage course through him. "No wonder your mother killed the bastard."

Brenna stared at their linked hands. "You know those books and movies where the mother is an irrepressible free spirit and the daughter is the wise one of the pair, the one who assumes the responsibility and all? Well, in books and movies, it ends well for both—the mother learns a lesson and finally grows up and the daughter gets to be a kid again, after all. But in real life it doesn't work out that way."

"No. I can see how it wouldn't."

"Everything was so different when I lived with my father," Brenna continued, as if reciting an old dream that she'd repeated many times. "Daddy married my mother because she was pregnant, and they were divorced shortly after I was born. My dad got custody of me, and I lived with him and his parents. Mom rarely visited. I have very few memories of her, until my dad and grandparents were killed in a car accident when I was six."

Luke wanted to say something comforting, something wise and profound, but he couldn't find the words. Her history chilled him. At six he'd been mischievous and carefree, secure within a big family, while she had faced the wreck of her whole world.

"Did you go to live with your mother then?"

"Yes. There was insurance money. Taking custody of me was the only way Mom could get her hands on it."

"Your mother sounds like a mean piece of work, Brenna."

"Marly described herself as zany and spontaneous,"

Brenna said wryly. "She couldn't understand why the rest of the world didn't acknowledge how special she was. I can remember her ranting about it. She was completely estranged from her own family. According to her, they were 'dull, hateful prudes.' My guess is that they were appalled by her and glad to cut the ties. I have no idea who they are or where to look for them, so I never have."

"And from the age of six you were essentially without protection, dragged along with your mother's parade of boyfriends?"

"I didn't like any of them, and they didn't like having me around, either. The only thing that made it bearable was my drawing."

Brenna smiled, a genuine smile of pleasure. "I started drawing when I was really little, and Daddy and Gramma and Gramps always encouraged me. By the time I started kindergarten, I had stacks of sketch books and boxes of colored pencils and pens. I could copy almost anything, and I used to entertain the kids at school by drawing pictures of cartoon characters. When I went to live with my mother, school became my refuge. All sixteen of them."

"You went to sixteen schools?" Luke was incredulous.

"Marly wasn't one to stay in the same place for very long. During the seven years I lived with her, I went to sixteen different schools, but thankfully, I made friends in all of them. My artwork was the key. As I got older, I could do original pictures instead of just copying things, so I'd draw the kids in class as whatever they wanted to be— superheroes, supermodels, even animals. Whatever. I drew the teachers and the mothers of my friends, too, and always made them look gorgeous. It was a surefire way to please people."

"But you were a just a child. A kid shouldn't have to go from school to school, learning how to ingratiate herself.

Geez, it's like a candidate running for office, always having to be likable while scrounging for votes.''

Brenna actually laughed. ''I guess it sort of is. Just think, if I hadn't been able to draw, I might've ended up as a politician.''

Luke didn't join in the laughter. He was thinking of his own school years. The same school from kindergarten through eighth grade, then the same high school for the next four years. His sisters, brothers, cousins and friends had all led the same structured, predictable lives.

So very different from Brenna's.

''Why did your mother keep moving?'' he pressed.

''She was constantly looking for a fresh start.'' Brenna heaved a sad, reminiscent sigh. ''But it was always the same for her, plunging into new relationships. She would meet a woman who would be her new best friend—until the inevitable blowout that ended the friendship within a few months, if not weeks. It was even worse with men, because she would fall madly in love, invite the new lover to move in or else move in with him, and then the fighting began and the breakup was bitter. The few times a man wanted to stick around and try to work things out, Mom was the one to end it, claiming she felt trapped.''

''She sounds nuts, Brenna!''

''She had a personality disorder, according to the court psychiatrists, but that isn't considered mental illness.'' Brenna grimaced. ''Mom didn't think there was anything wrong with her, ever. Even at her trial, she got on the stand and insisted that it was everybody's else's fault and she was the true victim.''

''I bet that went over big.''

''According to Mom, the jury and the judge all hated her, and so did her own attorney.'' Brenna shrugged. ''It could be true. I remember her attorney took me to lunch and bought me some art supplies and advised me to cut off contact with Mom when she went to prison. 'I know Marly's your mother but she's bad news,' he said.''

"Is your mother still in prison?"

"Yes. She got a life sentence and won't be eligible for parole until she's served twenty years."

Luke let out a low whistle. "For killing the man who raped her daughter? I'm no lawyer, but it seems like that might qualify as grounds for temporary insanity or some kind of manslaughter. And having to serve a full twenty years before becoming eligible for parole could be considered severe."

"The police and the prosecution didn't see it that way."

"Which means I'm not seeing the whole picture, just an incomplete outline of what actually happened," Luke concluded.

"It's such an ugly story, Luke."

"We don't have to take it any further if you don't want to, Brenna. But you've risen above whatever ugliness happened. Never lose sight of that fact."

Brenna gazed at him gratefully. He seemed to instinctively know when to encourage her to talk and when not to press her. She loved him for that, for his tact and his kindness to her.

She loved Luke Minteer—and along with that insight came the realization that loving him freed her to share the whole ugly truth with him.

"That night after he—" Brenna began to speak, but she never said the monster's name, not then and not now "—was done with me, he left, and I called a friend whose parents came and took me to the hospital. The ER nurse called the police to report it. I went home with my friends that night, and the next day I told my mother what happened. She didn't believe me. First she said I'd made it up, then she said I was the one who seduced him because I was jealous of her. When he came sneaking back a few nights later, she didn't call the police, she let him in. Greeted him with a smile and a kiss.''

Luke looked sick. "Brenna, what did you do?"

"I got out of there fast. I ran to my friend's house, and they called the police. But by the time they got to our place, Mom had already—done it."

"She'd killed him," Luke verified.

"Yes. Mom said he was drunk and told her about that night with me and said that I was—" Brenna paused and took a deep breath "—sexier than she was. Then he passed out and she loaded the gun and shot him. The D.A. said it was the insult to her ego that caused her to kill him, not any maternal concern for me. The jury agreed and convicted her of first-degree murder."

Luke said nothing, nothing at all.

"Yes, that part always renders people speechless." Brenna's tone was resigned. "It's so vile and trashy, I learned not to tell anybody. Because after the listeners recover enough to speak, they always say the same thing—'You poor thing.' And then there's more silence. I see either distance or pity in their eyes, and—"

"Brenna, if you see either distance or pity in my eyes, you're misinterpreting, because all I want to do is take you in my arms and hold you and try to make the pain go away."

Luke reached for her. Brenna drew back.

"The pain is gone, Luke. I dealt with it a long time ago."

"Did you, Brenna? Or is it still ruling your life?"

"I was very lucky and had a lot of help coping with it, Luke. After the trial, some of the parents of my friends at school arranged for me to be sent to Denver, a few hundred miles away, to a group home for girls who couldn't live with their families because of abuse or neglect. It was nondenominational but run by nuns, and the girls placed there had to meet certain qualifications—their grades had to be decent and they had to be considered at risk for getting into trouble but not delinquent. The hope was to show the girls who held promise that there were alternatives to…to the way they'd been living."

"And you fit the bill."

"Yes, fortunately for me, I went to live there."

"And while you were there, you made friends and loved school?" Luke guessed. His dark-blue eyes shone with affection.

"I was there until I graduated from high school, and I loved the discipline and the routine and the order. There was lots of warmth and encouragement and fun, too. I won a scholarship to art school and…well, I've just kept on drawing."

"So how did you end up here in Pennsylvania? It's a long way from Denver."

"I accepted a job with a commercial ad agency in Philadelphia two years ago. It was a good salary with benefits, and I thought I ought to at least try working for a company instead of freelancing. I moved there…and hated the job from the first day."

"You preferred being your own boss, setting your own hours," surmised Luke.

"I liked drawing what I wanted, the way I wanted too much, to conform to the company way. I also decided I wanted to leave Philadelphia for somewhere smaller."

"This area isn't particularly well known, even throughout the state, Brenna. How did you come to be here?" Luke asked curiously.

"One of my friends in Philadelphia was Angela Volario—you know, whose family owns the Italian market here. She talked about her hometown a lot, and I came along with her to visit one weekend. It seemed like a good place to live and raise a child, and I really wanted a family.

I'd gotten past my fears that I might turn out to be a mother like mine.''

"That will never happen, Brenna," Luke assured her. "Never."

"I know that now. The nuns said over and over that we have free will and make our own choices. I finally realized I wasn't doomed to be like Marly, that I'd had a good father and grandparents and friends and teachers I could emulate. I could be a good, loving parent."

"All true. But I'd bet my next contract advance that the nuns wouldn't wholeheartedly cheer your trip to the sperm bank and your plan to have this baby solo, without—"

"I haven't told them anything about it yet." Brenna averted her eyes. "When I take the baby back to Denver to visit—which I'm definitely going to do—I know they'll be happy for me. And they'll be proud that I'm such a good mother," she added, her eyes flashing, daring him to disagree.

"I have no doubt you'll be a great mother, Brenna."

Her brief show of defiance seemed to evaporate, without an argument to fire it. Her shoulders drooped; she appeared physically spent. Luke felt a surge of compassion for her. No wonder she didn't want to revisit her past—it was a grueling ordeal, too draining for a woman in her condition.

He cupped his hand around her nape and began a gentle massage. She leaned into it, closing her eyes.

"Has there ever been a man in your life, Brenna?" Luke asked softly.

"No. I was more interested in directing my thoughts and energy into my drawing. Having a boyfriend was never a priority to me."

"For *boyfriend,* substitute *poisonous snake*—or *sex-crazed rapist?*"

"I guess I do have a few issues still pending in that area."

"Yeah, your sperm bank visit is proof of that."

She smiled slightly. "It seemed like the ideal solution. A way to have a baby without having to endure sex to get one. Until I met you, I never even had the desire to—" She broke off and shook her head, her eyes gleaming. "You can see what a clueless numbskull I am in the male-female arena. Admitting to you—a notorious smooth operator—that you're the first and only man I've ever wanted is pretty pathetic."

She stood up and smoothed the wrinkles from her maternity top. "Feel free to ignore my lack of...cool, especially since a hormonal pregnant woman is hardly a—"

"I don't want to ignore it." Luke stood up, too. There was a sexy glint in his blue eyes. "And you know I think you're *cool*."

Brenna had to laugh at his inflection, at the word, at the strange circumstances they were in.

"I want to take you to bed and show you how much I want you, too, Brenna. I want to show you that there is nothing to endure. Are you ready to let me?"

"Yes," she breathed, her tone filled with both surprise and wonder. "I am, Luke."

Eight

They walked hand in hand to the staircase, pausing to kiss at the foot of the stairs.

"Do you want me to pick you up and carry you?" he asked, leaning toward her as if readying himself to do just that.

"Please don't. Maybe it's because of the baby, but being carried is—unnerving, Luke." Brenna swallowed. "I'm sorry."

"No apologies necessary." Luke put his arm around her and led her up the stairs. "I'll never make you do anything you don't want to, Brenna. You don't ever have to be afraid that I will."

She reached for his hand resting on her shoulder and linked her fingers with his. "So there will be no more pressure from you to name the baby Sam or Lucas, if it's a boy?" she teased, feeling playful and younger than she could ever remember feeling.

"Let me qualify my last statement. I'll never pressure you sexually. Otherwise, I'll try my damnedest to get you to do things my way. Winning over the opposition is part of my ex-political-operative charm."

They both laughed as they reached the top of the stairs and headed toward her bedroom. This time she felt no trepidation as he undressed her, she made no apologies for her pregnant figure. No apologies necessary, she reminded herself. Luke had seen her before, and he had stayed. He'd even made the return trip to her bedroom!

So when he told her how feminine and beautiful she was, Brenna allowed herself to believe that he meant what he was saying. That he believed it himself.

They kissed and caressed each other for a long time, with no sense of rush, no need to hurry things along. Each touch was special, each kiss meaningful, as tenderness and passion built and merged together into a loving conflagration.

They lay on the bed together until Luke helped her on top of him, to sit astride him, putting her in a position that paradoxically made her both vulnerable and powerful at the same time.

Brenna wanted more, more affection, more reassurance. More of him.

Leaning forward, she twined her fingers through the springy thickness of his hair. The sensitive tips of her breasts brushed his chest as she kissed him, her mouth open and demanding, hot and wild

Luke's hands skimmed along the length of her back, tracing the fine line of her spine and the small dimple at the base of it. After a few of these sweeping caresses, he cupped her buttocks, filling his palms with them and lushly squeezing.

She moaned her arousal and wriggled sensuously atop him, bringing her into full contact with his throbbing erection.

Luke reached up to fondle her breasts, teasing the nipples until she arched her back, tipping back her head so that her hair dangled down her back.

She closed her eyes as Luke lowered his hand and his clever fingers caressed her with an erotic expertise. Perspiration glowed on her skin as a primal instinct guided her into a position which most maximized the pleasure.

Brenna felt her body sinking into the sensual rhythm provided by his hand, and the delicious tension built, growing tighter, burning hotter. Her head lolled on her neck, frenetically turning from side to side, and her lips parted as she breathed his name and moaned her pleasure.

Her eyes remained tightly closed. Opening them would require too much effort, and her whole being was focused on what he was doing to her, what he was making her feel.

He murmured love words, sexy words that excited her even more. Luke was good with words; the thought flashed through her feverish brain. He was also very good with his hands.

She nearly smiled at the thought, except at that moment, he slowly, carefully inserted his finger inside her. First one, then another while his thumb maintained just the right amount of light pressure on the small swollen bud that ached and throbbed for his touch.

"You're close now." His voice was low and deep and seemed to exert a hypnotic effect on her.

"Yes. Please," she mumbled, as if in a trance.

"Please what, sweetheart?"

"You—you know." Her words were thick and almost incoherent.

"Tell me what you want, Brenna. And say my name," he added, a possessive note creeping into his tone.

Embarrassment and fear had lost all meaning; she felt sensual, she felt free. To say and do and feel. "Let me climax, Luke. Please."

"Yes, Brenna. I'll do anything for you."

And then he did, and a searing flash of heat exploded within her, making her writhe and rock and scream his name as her entire body convulsed with the power of her surrender.

It was a wondrous, rapturous tidal wave of heat and passion and release crashing over her. Before she could come down, as her body still quivered with aftershocks of pleasure, Brenna felt his big strong hands on her hips, settling her directly over him.

Guiding himself inside her.

She felt her body opening to his penetration, accepting him within her.

"That's it, sweetheart," he rasped. "I want you so much. You feel so good, so soft, like hot velvet. You're my love, and I'll never hurt you. You know that, don't you, Brenna? Don't ever be afraid of me."

Fear was the farthest thing from her mind, Brenna thought dizzily as she felt her body stretching to sheathe him. The fullness felt wonderful, an indescribable contrast to that empty ache that she'd known only since Luke had first aroused her. He was her first everything, and their bodies seemed exquisitely attuned to each other's.

Her insides pulsed thrillingly with his every rhythmic stroke. He adjusted her position once again until she could feel his manhood rub more directly against her most sensitive place.

"Better?" he muttered huskily.

Brenna saw shards of color streak like fireworks behind her closed eyelids. She whimpered. *Better* was definitely an understatement. It was the best, the most marvelous, the wildest and hottest...

And then their bodies both plunged over the precipice into a sublime free fall.

Luke held her as feelings he'd never experienced gripped

him. He'd had intercourse before, of course, but this was the first time it went beyond physical pleasure for him.

He felt as if Brenna had absorbed him as he had entered her, that the two of them had merged and become one. She was on top of him and he was inside her, he could taste her on his lips and feel her passion-slick skin against his own. A rush of protectiveness and pride swept through him. She was his.

Her body was trembling, and he could feel her delicate little shivers as he gently eased himself out of her.

He placed her down beside him, keeping her close and tucking her into the curve of his body, like nesting spoons. Smoothing a lock of her hair away from her cheek, he gently tucked it behind her ear.

He loved her. The insight struck him with the force of a two-by-four to the head, leaving him feeling slightly giddy. For the first time in his life, he was truly in love.

He guessed there might have been—there most certainly had been—a time in his life when, if someone had told him he would fall in love with an almost-nine-months-pregnant woman carrying another man's child, he would've laughed himself silly.

Of course, nobody would ever have said such a thing, because it was just too improbable for anybody to imagine. He was the Minteer with the best imagination, and not even he could have come up with a scenario more unlikely than this one.

But it had happened, and Luke decided he wouldn't have it any other way. He wanted Brenna, only Brenna, and if she happened to be almost nine months pregnant, that's how he wanted her. Just the way she was.

His hand automatically came to rest on Brenna's abdomen, where the baby lay quiescent within her womb. Never mind the med student who'd biologically fathered this child via the sperm bank—the man whom this child called "Daddy" was going to be Luke Minteer.

"Luke?" she murmured, her voice quavering.

"I'm here, honey." He kissed the corner of her jaw, her earlobe, the curve of her neck.

"Could you go home now?"

It took a while for him to fully process what she'd just said. When it finally dawned...

"You're kicking me out?" Luke was staggered. "You're not only kicking me out of your bed, you're kicking me out of your house?"

"I want to be by myself. Please, Luke." Her voice rose to a nervous plea. "I really need some time alone."

"Tough." His hands drifted over her body, caressing, soothing, apologizing for his stand. But not reconsidering. "You've already spent too much time by yourself, Brenna. Now I'm with you, and I'm staying with you. Deal with it."

"Oh, I've done it now, haven't I?" Brenna groaned. "You've taken my request as a challenge and decided to stay put."

"It wasn't a request, it was an order, and you can't say you weren't warned about what would happen." Luke nipped her shoulder, then laved it with his tongue. "A less secure man might go running off, but luckily I have a strong male ego and am not taking your attempted rejection personally."

Within his embrace, Brenna rolled onto her other side, facing him, her arm sliding reflexively across his middle. She regarded him gravely for a moment. Her lashes were spiky with tears, her eyes shimmered with them.

"There are those who might say your ego is more than merely strong, it's overinflated, which makes you overbearing. And that you should take my attempted rejection personally because—well, what could be more personal

than a woman kicking you out of her bed right after...
after—'' She bit her lip and shook her head, unable to
continue.

Luke lifted her hand to his mouth and kissed each finger,
punctuating his words with the light touches of his lips.

"After we made love and you loved every minute of it?"
he suggested.

Brenna flinched.

"You're absolutely right, you know," Luke continued
calmly. "There are those who would say all those things
you just said. But I have a thick skin. So even though you
feel compelled to say stuff to send me away, I can just
shrug it off. And I'll stay with you, just like you want me
to, Brenna."

She glowered at him. "What do I have to say to get you
to go away and leave me alone?"

"Your body language is saying all I need to know,
honey."

Brenna glanced down at her arm, draped across his stomach, at her leg which had slipped between his.... She hadn't
even realized what she'd done. It was as if her limbs had
moved of their own volition in direct opposition to her
stated demands.

"So I've come to this—saying one thing and doing another," she said grimly. "Which makes me a total nutcase
who is—"

"You're not nuts and you're not hormonal," Luke cut
in, his voice ringing with that confidence and assurance he
projected so well. "Your mother was a wacko and surrounded herself with similar kinds, which meant that you
had to endure too many of them during those rotten years
with her. So you learned not to let your guard down, and
it's hard to break old defensive habits. That's all it is,
Brenna."

"It's hard to argue with someone who's arguing that you're not crazy." Brenna's voice was tinged with irony.

"Yeah, it is. So stop arguing and go to sleep."

"Will you be here in the morning?" Brenna's heart hammered wildly in her chest.

"I'll be here, Brenna."

He didn't say anything else, and neither did she.

Was Luke right? Brenna wondered, confused. Did she really want him to stay here with her?

Already she was beginning to reconstruct those invisible walls around her heart. She reminded herself how much she cherished her privacy and how much time alone she required.

As for sharing a bed all night with him...well, that wasn't going to happen. It couldn't. At the school in Denver, she'd had a terrible time sleeping while sharing a *room* with another girl and hadn't shared a room with anyone since. Let alone a bed.

Brenna tried not to think of what she'd done with Luke today. Her mind was already on overload. Reliving the wild, hot memories would probably short-circuit it! But try as she might to suppress them, those feelings sneaked past her guard, evoking everything.

What they'd done. What they'd said. How wonderful it all had been.

And he was still here, holding her in the dark silence of her room, warming her with his body heat. His steady breathing echoed in her ears. It was a calming, reassuring sound.

She would lie here for just a little longer and then convince him to leave.

But wrapped in Luke's arms, Brenna felt as if her tired mind and her satiated body were floating away as she slowly drifted into sleep.

"The good news is that it's stopped snowing and the roads have been cleared," Luke announced the next morning.

Brenna, who'd awakened moments earlier, struggled to a sitting position in bed and watched him look out the window.

He was dressed in his clothes from yesterday, but his face was smoothly shaven and his hair still damp from the shower. He looked vigorous and alert and cheerful—whereas she felt nowhere near any of those enviable states.

"The bad news is that it's stopped snowing and the roads have been cleared—and everything is open and running on time today," Luke continued. "I heard it on the radio, which means we have jury duty today. Ready for another go-round of Gimme That Ring?"

Brenna closed her eyes and tried to stifle a moan. She didn't quite succeed.

"My sentiments exactly." Luke chuckled. "When we jurors get together to deliberate, I'm going to suggest that the court confiscate the damn ring and donate it to charity."

Should she try to explain that it wasn't the prospect of serving on the jury and listening to Amber's and Brad's attorneys do their best to portray each other's clients as greedy/stingy, shameless/shameful wretches who did/did not deserve the diamond ring?

No, it was the thought of having to sit next to Luke Minteer in the jury box all day, and wondering what to say and do after the courtroom session ended.

Brenna gnawed nervously on her lower lip.

Suppose he asked—no, Luke didn't ask, he just did as he pleased—and suppose it pleased him to come back to her house with her again tonight? To make love to her and spend the night with her again? Why, she'd intended to send him on his way last night—except she'd fallen asleep first.

And for it to occur two nights in a row? She couldn't handle so much intimacy. Brenna shivered. The very idea made her claustrophobic.

But suppose it didn't please him to be with her? Suppose yesterday had been both the beginning and the end of her involvement with Luke Minteer?

She couldn't handle that, either!

For the first time in her life, Brenna felt a sharp flicker of recognition. This awful uncertainty must have been what her mother's chaotic romantic life had been like.

Brenna was aghast. She had spent years avoiding men to save herself from falling into the same traps that had constantly ensnared her mother. Yet here she was, so like Marly, falling in love and into bed with a man she hadn't known long enough. Wasting her time and brain cells worrying about what would happen next. Would he call? Wouldn't he? What did every nuance of his every word and expression mean?

Brenna steeled herself against it. She would *not* subject herself or her baby to any of that futile nonsense.

"You went into the bathroom about four times last night," Luke said.

Brenna's eyes flew open, and she felt a hot blush spread over every inch of her skin. She saw Luke studying her, and she didn't meet his eyes. She couldn't. The physical intimacy they'd shared last night didn't extend to this morning—nor to pointed observations on her bathroom habits!

"Was it because you're so far along in the pregnancy or because of the sex?" Luke's brows narrowed in concern.

"The pregnancy," Brenna replied brusquely. "I've been getting up a lot at night for the past month or so." She threw off the covers and swung her legs over the side of the bed.

She was naked, a fact she'd forgotten. Looking down at

herself while making an ungainly escape into the sanctuary of the bathroom made her cringe.

But she made a successful, if ungainly, escape to the sanctuary of the bathroom, closed the door and locked it.

"I'll make some breakfast," Luke called through the door. "What do you want?"

"Anything. Whatever you're going to have." She turned on the shower, and the roaring sound of the water precluded any further conversation.

After a quick breakfast of juice and cereal, they drove to the courthouse in silence. There had been an argument about taking two cars. Brenna insisted on driving herself. Luke said it made no sense as parking was sure to be scarce since the snowplows had been utilized to clear the district's roads, not the parking lots. However, the VIP spots in front of the courthouse would surely be cleared.

Why should Brenna drive around town, searching for what might be a nonexistent parking space? Luke argued. Even if she found one, there would be a long cold walk to the courthouse, and the sidewalks might be slippery. If she fell, she could hurt herself or the baby.

Brenna accused him of being manipulative for bringing the baby into this. Luke replied it was impossible not to bring the baby into this, as it was inside her.

In the end Brenna decided it was easier simply to ride to the courthouse with Luke. His points were too valid to ignore. Besides, she could tell he wasn't going to budge on the issue. He assured her that he wouldn't, and she'd come to realize that he always meant what he said.

Luke swung the Dodge Durango into the cleared VIP spot directly in front of the courthouse, came around to her side and lifted her out of the truck.

"There's just one thing," Brenna said, as he set her on the ground.

She was breathless from being handled by him and wanted nothing more than to lean into him and tuck her hand into his. But she kept it at her side.

"And what's that?" Luke reached for her hand and slipped it into his pocket, pulling her closer to him in the process.

Brenna felt his body brush hers and a honeyed warmth oozed through her. "I want to go right home after we're finished here for the day."

"Okay, I'll take you right home," he replied easily.

"And—I don't want you to come into my house or ask if you can. Because my answer will be no," she finished in a rush.

"Well, I guess this is one of those damned-if-you-do or damned-if-you-don't situations." He sounded more resigned than angry or sad. "If I agree to drop you off without any protest, you'll assume I want to leave you. If I refuse and insist on coming in with you, you'll accuse me of stalking you. Of not knowing how to take no for an answer."

"You *don't* know how to take no for an answer. I don't have to *prove* that," she added.

Even to her own ears she sounded cranky and ill-tempered. She really wouldn't blame Luke if he dropped her hand and stomped off inside the courthouse.

Instead, Luke laughed. They kept on walking together, up the stairs and into the building.

In the jury box, the jurors exchanged tales of yesterday's storm and how they'd weathered it. Everybody but Luke and Brenna complained about the lack of accessible parking spaces since the lots had only been partially plowed.

Brad and Amber and their attorneys sat at their respective tables, ignoring each other.

Everybody rose when the judge entered the courtroom.

"Your Honor, yesterday afternoon the Pennsylvania Su-

preme Court upheld a ruling by the Superior Court that
pertains to this case," Brad's lawyer announced, looking
very pleased. "If I may cite the ruling…"

Brad, clearly aware of what was to come, grinned from
ear to ear.

Amber's lawyer looked as if he knew, too. He grimaced
and seemed to brace himself as he whispered something in
his client's ear.

"Amber looks ready to hit something, or somebody,
probably Brad or his lawyer," Luke whispered to Brenna.
"Maybe both."

The judge, giving nothing away by his expression, told
Brad's attorney to continue.

"In a case with circumstances closely paralleling this
one, the Superior Court ordered the fiancée to give back
the engagement ring after the engagement was terminated,"
the lawyer continued in a majestic baritone. "The Superior
Court considered this case to be a 'case of first impression.'"

He turned to the jury and added in an aside, "That means
the Court's ruling would be the standard for similar cases
in the future."

"I read the ruling, Counselor," chimed in the judge.
"The Supreme Court justices said that the state had adopted
a no-fault divorce statute back in 1980 and should apply
similar principles to cases spawned by broken engage-
ments."

"It's long overdue for these personal issues of blame and
fault to be removed from the courtroom, Your Honor,"
Brad's attorney said smugly.

The judge shot him a warning look. "I hereby order the
ring returned and dismiss this case."

"No!" shrieked Amber, jumping to her feet. "That's not
fair!"

"Sit down and be quiet, young lady," ordered the judge,

pounding his gavel. He turned to the jury. "The jurors are dismissed with the Commonwealth's thanks for performing your civic duty."

"They didn't do anything but sit there and stare at me!" howled Amber.

"You see why I broke up with her?" Brad addressed the jury himself. "Would any of you guys want to marry her?"

"She's pretty hot, though," one Jason chortled to the other.

After another pound of the gavel and another demand for silence, the judge departed. The attorneys attempted to shepherd their bickering clients from the courtroom as Amber cursed furiously at the preening, triumphant Brad.

The jurors filed out of the jury box.

"Let's go before we're witnesses to a homicide and have to come back to testify," joked one of the older women.

Beside her, Brenna felt Luke freeze in place. She glanced up at him to see him staring down at her, a look of concern on his face.

"Brenna, what she said..." Luke murmured. "She didn't know about your—"

"I know," Brenna said quietly. "I don't take jokes like that personally." Her lips tightened. "But when it comes to books that make crime seem exciting and criminals seem interesting, *those* I take those personally."

Roger, the jury's elected foreman, invited everybody to Peglady's to celebrate their unexpected freedom.

"Do you want to go?" Luke asked Brenna.

She shook her head. "I want to go home. Alone!"

"Anything you want, you've got it," said Luke. Then he hummed a few bars of it.

As she'd requested—demanded!—Luke drove directly to her house. He politely assisted her to the front door, and when Brenna opened it, he made no move to come inside.

Her heart sinking, she watched him stroll back down the walk. This was the way she wanted it, Brenna reminded herself sternly.

It was just that she didn't want him to want it that way, too! Brenna realized she was on the verge of tears. She fought against them, appalled by her weakness.

"Do you want me to pick you up at six or six-thirty for dinner tonight?" Luke called to her, just before he climbed behind the wheel.

The jolt of relief she felt was palpable, throwing her so off balance that she feared she would lose her already tenuous control and start to cry, if she attempted to speak.

Oh, the effect of all these hormones, causing her moods to shift crazily from low to high!

Or was it the effect of Luke Minteer?

"Okay, six it is," Luke answered for her. "See you then, Brenna."

Nine

Luke's phone was ringing as he walked into his house. It was cold inside, and he kept his coat on. All those hours without electrical power gave the place the ambience of an igloo.

He made it to the phone just before his answering machine was set to pick up. And was astonished to find Steve Saraceni, a Harrisburg lobbyist and pal from his bad old days in the state capital, on the other end of the line.

"Hey, Luke. Hope I'm not interrupting your perp in the middle of slicing and dicing his latest victim," joked Steve.

Luke tried to recall the last time he'd talked to Steve Saraceni. Probably while he was still working for Matt and living in D.C., wheeling and dealing in the world of politics. Among other things.

None of which explained why the lobbyist was calling him now.

"What can I do for you, Steve?" Luke was curious.

"For me? Nothing, actually. I'm calling because my sister called me earlier today and—" Steve paused and cleared his throat. "I guess I should explain that my sister, Cassie Walsh, lives next door to a, um, a friend of yours. A *very special* friend of yours."

"My very special friend," Luke repeated, putting together the pieces.

It seemed that Steve Saraceni's sister had done some piece fitting herself—and Luke's instincts told him that she'd come up with the wrong picture.

"Oh, damn, Luke, we've known each other too long and too well for me not to come straight to the point. Cassie is irate because she says you're the father of this girl's unborn baby, and not only do you refuse to take responsibility, but for months you've been pretending you didn't even know her. According to Cassie, this young mother-to-be has to deal with everything, including all expenses, completely on her own."

Luke sank down on a chair, clutching the phone. His instincts had been right on target.

"Luke, are you still there?"

Steve's voice seemed to reverberate in Luke's head. "Yeah, I'm here."

"Go ahead, tell me it's none of my business." Steve heaved a sigh. "Because I know it isn't. I just wanted to—well, I wanted to find out if it's true, or if my sister might have misconstrued things."

"And why would she do that, Steve?"

"This girl is pregnant and Cassie saw her with you, the only man who's ever even visited her. She found the girl crying after you left, and you've spent the night over there."

"And that's all the evidence?" Luke drawled. "Don't know if you could indict me with that, Steve."

"I know. Cassie is a sweetheart, but she gets downright

militant on the subject of fathers' responsibilities toward kids. She had a bad experience with her sons' deadbeat dad and can be evangelical about looking out for...for—''

''—children whose fathers abandon them?'' Luke filled in. ''Who can blame her? Certainly not me.''

''You still haven't denied anything, Luke,'' Steve pointed out. ''You've done some dodging and weaving but no denying.''

''And we both know that a nondenial might as well be a blatant confirmation. I might not be playing anymore, but I haven't forgotten the rules of the game, Steve,'' Luke added with a wry, reminiscent chuckle.

''So it's true, then?'' Steve audibly gulped. ''You and this girl are—''

''Her name is Brenna. And your sister is right about Brenna being pregnant. She's due within a month.''

There was a long silence. When Steve spoke again, his characteristic silky-smooth tone held a distinctly disapproving note. ''You're pretty cavalier about the whole thing, Minteer. Does your brother know?''

''Matt? Of course not. Until now, nobody in Harrisburg knew, either. But you're about to change that situation, right, Steve?'' Luke gave a sharp laugh. ''After all, we also both know that in the political world, information is valuable currency. And you know how to spend it better than anybody.''

''Same old Luke,'' Steve said, with a touch of malice. ''Don't say I didn't check for the facts first. And I promise that I'll spend this *currency* to the best of my ability.'' Then he hung up.

Which meant that there would be a discreet, immediate phone call placed to Congressman Matthew Minteer's office in D.C. from Steve Saraceni himself.

Luke could almost hear the oh-so-congenial-and-concerned lobbyist say to his brother, ''Just wanted to give you a heads-up on a certain rumor circulating in your district, Matt.''

In this district of traditional values and strong family ties, rumors of a Minteer getting a young woman pregnant and then leaving her to fend for herself would go over about as well as a nude orgy on a church lawn.

Congressman Minteer would be indebted to Steve Saraceni for tipping him off in time to do some damage control, and in the political world a personal debt was golden. Even better than information.

Same old Luke. The phrase echoed in Luke's head.

Except he *wasn't* the same old Luke. That Luke, the one Steve Saraceni had known, would have had nothing to do with a pregnant Brenna Morgan in the first place. Apart from the obligatory hello and goodbye bestowed on all his fellow jurors, the same old Luke would not have bothered talking to Brenna at all.

Thus forever missing his chance with the woman whom he knew was irrefutably the love of his life.

Of course, the same old Luke wouldn't have cared, because he had been seeking other things, like power and thrills. He hadn't been looking for love in his life.

Just as Brenna wasn't looking for love in hers. Not from a man, anyway. She was having a baby to love and to love her. Which was fine, but she needed more and so did the baby.

They both needed him—the new improved Luke Minteer—the man who had been redeemed by love.

He would do anything he had to do in order to become a part of their lives, Luke vowed. And he wouldn't settle for some vague peripheral role; he wanted nothing less than a vital, dynamic position with Brenna and Baby.

''Begin at the beginning'' was his brother Matt's mantra, when faced with a seemingly insurmountable political hurdle.

Well, the first step was getting Brenna to realize that they belonged together—which might not prove as easy as he wished.

But it was not an insurmountable hurdle. No such thing existed for the Minteers. They inevitably prevailed. And fortunately, he'd retained just enough tenacity, including a bit of underhandedness, from the same old Luke to achieve his goal.

Brenna was in that trancelike state she achieved when deeply immersed in creating the world where her paper dolls came to life. Everything in her own life faded deep into the background of her mind as she concentrated on the drawing paper in front of her.

Ideas came easily, and her fingers deftly sketched and measured and colored as characters appeared, accompanied by their individual histories and characteristics, their wardrobes and possessions.

She completed the little boy Simon and moved into the next decade, the twenties, drawing Peggy, a child with bobbed hair and dresses with dropped waistlines similar to the flappers of that era.

She'd already thought ahead to the thirties. There definitely would have to be another little girl, one with Shirley Temple curls and short, frilly dresses to define that decade.

Each little paper-doll girl, Peggy and the Shirley lookalike, would have a doll with matching dresses. There should be pets, too, but what animal? She'd drawn so many cats and dogs over the years; it would be fun to do something else.

Would her editor think a parrot or a monkey was too exotic for a child in the twenties or thirties to own?

The doorbell rang several times before the sound registered with Brenna. She frowned at the intrusion. It always took her a moment or two to totally return to her life away from her books.

The first thing she noticed was the clock on the wall. It was just after five.

And then everything came back to her in a rush. Luke, his insistence on picking her up for dinner at—hadn't he said six o'clock?

Her heartbeat accelerated to warp speed, and Brenna tried to mock herself into staying cool and calm. After all, she wasn't a dizzy teenager eagerly waiting for her first boyfriend to pick her up for their big date! Why must she feel like one?

In spite of her resolve, Brenna stopped in the bathroom and checked herself in the mirror. Her hair needed brushing, and she brushed it. Her cheeks were already flushed, which eliminated any need for more color. Her eyes were bright, too bright. Brenna wondered how she could make them stop glowing.

And before she could stop herself, she applied a light coat of pink lipstick.

Reminding herself that it wasn't safe for the baby if she dashed down the stairs, that falling was a possible risk, Brenna forced herself to walk down the staircase slowly and carefully, holding on to the handrail.

The doorbell rang again, and she opened the door, expecting to see Luke.

She planned to tell him that she hadn't consented to this dinner date, plus he was almost an hour early for it. Drop-in visitors were unacceptable, a detriment to her work schedule. She hated being unexpectedly interrupted. Furthermore...

Brenna stared at the three women standing on her small porch. There was an older woman, probably sixty-something, and two younger ones, perhaps in their late twenties or very early thirties, all bundled in heavy coats.

They stared back at her.

"Sweet saints in heaven, it's true," the older woman murmured, her eyes sweeping over Brenna's very pregnant figure.

Brenna, suddenly self-conscious, straightened her long, pale-pink maternity sweater, tugging it farther over her maternity jeans.

"Of course it's true, Mom!" exclaimed one of the younger women, the tall, dark-haired, blue-eyed one who looked a lot like Luke. "As soon as Lisa told me, I knew it had to be true. Why would Cassie make up something like that?"

Brenna's eyes darted to the older woman with the same blue eyes and fair skin as her daughter. Her dark hair was heavily streaked with gray.

"I don't think we've met." Brenna managed to get the words out and was once again inordinately grateful to the nuns, who had stressed good manners so long and so often they'd become truly ingrained.

She extended her hand, which, to her consternation, was shaking. "I'm Brenna Morgan."

"Anne Marie Minteer," said the dark-haired young woman, clasping her hand. "Taylor," she added, almost as an afterthought. "This is my mother, Rosemary Minteer, and my sister-in-law Lisa. She's married to my brother John."

"Annie and I went to high school together," Lisa, a petite blonde, put in helpfully. "And my son, David, goes to preschool with your little neighbor Abigail Walsh. Her mom, Cassie, and I have become good friends this year. David and Abby like to play together."

Lisa seemed to run out of steam at that point and lapsed into silence.

"I've heard Cassie mention David," Brenna said politely, still mystified as to why the three were here. "Abby's mentioned him, too, I believe. The Walshes live right next door," she added, and pointed to their house, right next door.

Just in case the trio had come to the wrong place by mistake.

But the three women made no attempt to leave. Instead, Rosemary Minteer moved toward Brenna and attempted to put her arms around her.

"Brenna, you poor dear sweet girl."

Reflexively Brenna backed away in alarm. "What...what do you want?"

"You don't have to pretend with us, honey." Rosemary's blue eyes were filled with sadness and sympathy. "There is no need for you to stay silent any longer."

"Cassie told me today when we picked up the kids at preschool. I called John and Anne Marie and a few others right away," Lisa said earnestly.

"Please don't think that we blame you, Brenna," exclaimed Anne Marie. "None of us do, honest! We want you to know we're all firmly on your side in this."

"Everybody knows, my dear, so there is no reason for any more secrecy," chimed in Rosemary. "Why, I'd just hung up the phone from talking to Anne Marie when my sister-in-law Eileen called me. Her Patrick said he simply couldn't stay silent any longer, he said he didn't feel right keeping such a secret from the family. So he told his parents, and of course they called us right away."

"And Matt called Mom from D.C. a little while ago," Anne Marie said, glancing from Brenna to her mother. "He got the word straight from Harrisburg. The gossip isn't all over the district yet, though it soon will be, of course. But when you and Luke get—"

"Luke," Brenna repeated.

It was the only name among all those mentioned—aside from Cassie and Abigail Walsh—that held any relevance for her. She was still baffled about what her uninvited guests were talking about.

What did "everybody" know?

For one grim moment Brenna thought of her past, of her mother and the trial and that terrifying night with the monster who had set it all in motion. If everybody knew all about that, she couldn't remain in town.

Been there, done that! Starring as the object in a sordid round of gossip was something she did not care to repeat, and she would not subject her child to it, not even as an infant.

But logic quickly prevailed, and Brenna discarded that premise.

They'd cited Cassie Walsh as a source, and Cassie knew nothing about her past. And was the Patrick who'd been mentioned Luke's cousin, the young police officer? Patrick Minteer knew nothing about her, either, except that she had been in Luke's SUV and they'd had an argument....

Brenna tilted her head, assessing the two taller women with their piercing blue-eyed stares.

"Are you Luke's mother and sister?" Brenna surmised. Lisa's identity as an in-law, married to John Minteer, had already been confirmed.

"Goodness, didn't we explain who we are?" Rosemary shook her head. "I'm sorry, honey. It's just that this news was so unexpected, so out of the blue, that I guess we're not quite back to ourselves yet. Yes, I am Luke's mother, and Anne Marie is his younger sister. We're delighted to meet you, Brenna, but I can't help but wish we had met under more, well, conventional circumstances."

"As if Luke has ever been conventional!" Anne Marie rolled her eyes.

A sharp blast of icy wind whirled around them, and Lisa shivered. "Could we come inside?" she asked.

Since Lisa's teeth were practically chattering, and her

lips were purple from the cold, Brenna reluctantly ushered the three women into her house.

She didn't know what they wanted with her, and she really, *really* didn't want to have to entertain them. Still, she refrained from suggesting that they go back to where they'd come from.

Etiquette drills aside, they were Luke's relatives.

Plus, they didn't look as if they would be any easier to evict than Luke himself, if determined to stay. Brenna suppressed a sigh.

"Would you like some tea?" she asked, silently mocking herself.

She had slipped effortlessly back into her people-pleasing ways. What next? Asking if they would like her to draw paper dolls of their children? How had Luke described her how-to-win-friends behavior during her school-girl years?

Ingratiating. And that description fit her right now, too— the ingratiating Brenna Morgan.

"We'd love some tea," Rosemary said, and they followed Brenna, single file, into the kitchen.

All three Minteer women exclaimed over everything they passed along the way—the carpeting, the pictures on the walls, the color of the walls. Even the overhead light fixture!

They marveled over her exquisite taste in everything.

Brenna had to smile. It appeared that she wasn't the only one who was being ingratiating this evening.

She prepared the tea while the three Minteers continued to enthuse over everything in her kitchen, as if Brenna were the most inventive, tasteful decorator since Martha Stewart. Which, of course, she was not.

It would've been comical, if she hadn't sensed the undercurrent of tension in the trio—which actually seemed more like a riptide than a current, Brenna concluded. What was really going on here?

She arranged the mugs of tea and the cream and sugar on a tray to carry to the table for them.

"How handy that you have a tray!" squealed Lisa with abject delight. "And the sugar bowl matches the little cream pitcher. You have such flair, Brenna!"

She had flair because she owned a tray and a matching sugar bowl and creamer? It was just too much. Brenna began to grow exceedingly alarmed. Something was *very* wrong, and she couldn't wait another second to find out.

She turned to Luke's mother with wide, questioning eyes. "Please tell me why you're here," she said bluntly, throwing ingratiation to the wind.

"Brenna, it's time to end the pretense." Rosemary met her gaze squarely. "We *all* know...your neighbors the Walshes, the entire Minteer family. We know you're carrying Luke's baby."

"Carrying Luke's baby?" Brenna echoed incredulously. "How did you come up with that?"

"Cassie *told* me that she probably wouldn't admit it," Lisa said knowingly. "Cassie said Brenna has kept her relationship with Luke so secret that she wasn't even aware the two of them knew each other, until they were both summoned for jury duty."

"But we didn't know each other till then," Brenna interjected.

Lisa and Anne Marie exchanged glances laden with disbelief.

"Brenna, there's no further need for this...charade," Anne Marie said with Luke-ish firmness. "Cassie told Lisa how you asked her questions about Luke your first day of jury duty—to carefully establish that you didn't know him. She said that looking back on that day now, she realized that you were nervous and clearly trying to hide something.''

Brenna thought back to that day when she'd quizzed Cassie for information about Luke Minteer. She actually had been trying to hide something—her unexpected attraction to Luke. And that really had made her nervous!

But Cassie and the Minteers had drawn the wrong conclusions all the way down the line.

''You're putting one and one together and getting three!'' Brenna protested.

''Exactly.'' Rosemary nodded vigorously. ''There are three of you. The baby and you and that...that son of mine. Oh, Luke has disgraced the family before, but never, ever to this degree! This time, he's taken *everything* we believe in and hold sacred and he has—''

''Blown it off,'' supplied Anne Marie.

''Yes,'' agreed her mother. ''I'm heartsick. For a son of mine to bully a defenseless young woman into silence after making her pregnant—because he doesn't want to get married—just sickens me.''

''Luke has made his opinions on marriage very clear at every wedding.'' Lisa frowned. ''He tried to talk John out of marrying me because he said John was too young to lock on the old ball and chain!''

Brenna could almost hear Luke saying it, his dark brows arched, his tone droll. ''It does sound like one of his jokes,'' she murmured.

''No, he wasn't joking,'' insisted Anne Marie. ''Luke tried to talk all of us into waiting to get married. He suggested waiting decades!''

Which only proved to Brenna that he really had been kidding—a suggestion to wait *decades* to wed was clearly a joke—but this time she declined to say so. The verdict was in, and the Minteer family jury had already pronounced Luke guilty of being anti-marriage.

''Though we don't like it, we've learned to live with Luke's smart-aleck attitude toward marriage and family,'' Rosemary continued darkly, ''but for him to blithely disregard the welfare of his own child and its mother is completely unacceptable. Now that we know the truth, we won't passively stand by and let that happen.''

Rosemary's voice rose with every word, and her face turned crimson. Brenna knew it wasn't physically possible for a person's head to explode, but if it were, at that particular moment, Rosemary Minteer's head would have detonated right there in her kitchen.

Yet all the furious disapproval was based on a false premise! Brenna hastened to set things straight.

''This isn't Luke's fault. Please don't be mad at him!'' Brenna implored.

She thought of how he'd come back to his hometown in disgrace after his D.C. antics, determined to win back his family's favor, of how hard he'd worked to regain their acceptance, showing up at every family occasion, happy and sad, boring or fun.

Oh, he made jokes about it, but Brenna knew how much his family meant to Luke. To have him branded an outcast again, this time over something that was not even his fault, was too much to bear.

She couldn't let that happen to him!

''You have no reason to be mad at Luke,'' she added more forcefully.

''No reason?'' Anne Marie gaped at her. ''Brenna, as much as it pains me to say it, because he is my own brother, Luke is a snake! The way he's treated you is terrible! Carrying on a secret affair and carelessly getting you pregnant! Then not even acknowledging his own baby, telling you to pretend you don't even know him and letting you handle the—''

''You don't understand!'' Brenna interrupted, feeling

frantic. As much as she valued her privacy, she couldn't let this falsehood go unchecked.

"You have it all wrong! Luke isn't the father of my baby! I...I went to a sperm bank. In Philadelphia. That's where I got pregnant. Luke had nothing to do with it."

Though she hadn't wanted to broadcast her child's origins—and telling the Minteers something seemed akin to announcing it over the airwaves—Brenna felt relief when she admitted the truth. She couldn't let Luke's family ostracize him when he was completely innocent of their accusations.

Brenna leaned back in her chair and closed her eyes, feeling drained, yet filled with a sense of conviction. She knew she'd done the right thing by sparing Luke another bout of Minteer condemnation.

Total silence followed her announcement. When Brenna raised her head and looked around the table, she saw that the three women watching her didn't seem at all placated and relieved by the truth.

They looked more enraged than before!

"A sperm bank?" snapped Rosemary. "In Philadelphia? Oh, that sounds exactly like Luke Minteer, all right. Mr. Big Shot Storyteller himself!"

"I can almost hear him saying it," said Anne Marie, blue eyes flashing. "He'd go, 'Hey, Brenna, if anybody should find out, say you went to a sperm bank—in Philadelphia because it's too big and far away for anybody to try to check out facts.' He thinks we're dummies!"

"Luke believes he is so clever, but I can see right through him," added Rosemary, her voice, her face, taut with fury.

"How could Luke be so cruel?" Lisa was distressed.

"Luke isn't cruel!" cried Brenna. Impulsively she reached over and grasped Rosemary's wrist. "And you don't see him at all if you can't see that he is a kind and loving person who has been patient and understanding and—''

"Are you sure you're talking about *our* Luke?" Anne Marie looked nonplussed. "Luke Minteer? Because nobody has ever described him in those terms. And as his family, we know him best.''

"As his family, you don't know him at all," Brenna countered fiercely. "Luke is incapable of making up a big lie to shirk responsibility for a child, especially if it were his own.''

"Poor thing, Luke really has you snowed," Anne Marie said, not unkindly. "But if you—''

"This conversation is pointless." Brenna stood up. "I don't want to be ungracious, but I would appreciate it if you would all leave now.''

She stalked out of the kitchen, an unmistakable cue for them to follow her to the door. It didn't matter how well-meaning they thought they were or how rude they thought she was, Brenna just wanted them gone.

It was quite a shock to find herself face-to-face with Luke in the hall. His winter jacket hung open, revealing a light-gray sweater and a pair of dark-gray cords.

Brenna came to an abrupt standstill. Her heart seemed to stand still, too.

"What are you—how did you—'' she stammered.

"The door was unlocked so I let myself in.'' Luke reached out to touch her, but Brenna quickly stepped back, out of range. "After I'd talked to my brother Matt, I thought I ought to head over here, although it's a little early for our dinner date.''

By now his mother, sister and sister-in-law had crowded into the small hallway with them.

"Looks like this particular triumvirate beat me here though,'' Luke added. His smile, his tone, were undeniably baiting.

Brenna gazed at the wicked gleam in his blue eyes, at the way his teeth flashed white against his shadowed jaw, which had been clean shaven in the morning.

He'd once mentioned that if he were going to some special function in the evening, he had to shave twice a day. Brenna found the notion exotic—sexy and virile, too.

And when she realized the path her thoughts were taking—while three outraged Minteer women stood there looking at Luke as if he were a vampire they'd like to stake—she wondered if she was beginning a slow descent into madness.

One thing was certain. Though Brenna felt herself beginning to succumb, his relatives were plainly not charmed by his teasing or by that devilish grin. Cold-eyed and scowling, they did not stop glaring at him.

"How long have you been here, Luke?" Anne Marie demanded crossly.

"Long enough to hear the sperm bank story," admitted Luke. He closed the gap between him and Brenna, and this time when he reached over and laid his hand on her shoulder, she didn't move away.

"I told you they'd never buy it, honey. The sperm bank part alone stretched credibility—but placing it in *Philadelphia?*" He made the city sound as remote as an outpost in Siberia. "That boosted it into the realm of the preposterous, Minteerwise. Nah, I knew that tale wouldn't play in this town—and especially not in this family."

For the first time since she'd met them, Brenna saw doubt and bewilderment on the Minteer women's faces.

"Luke Minteer, if you knew about—" his mother said, then gave her head a shake and started over. "Why in the name of God would you—" She broke off again, this time focusing those intense blue eyes of hers on Brenna rather than Luke.

"Is he saying *he* didn't make up that...that sperm-bank-in-Philadelphia nonsense?'' Rosemary directed her question to Brenna, as if she didn't trust Luke to answer honestly.

Brenna felt a flare of resentment on Luke's behalf, and momentarily forgot she was annoyed with him herself for his faux I-told-you-so. ''Mr. Big Shot Storyteller himself,'' his mother had called him. And she was 100 percent wrong!

''Of course he didn't make it up. Luke wouldn't do that.'' A reluctant smile quirked the corners of Brenna's lips. ''He'd rather rub the unpleasant truth in someone's face than make up some face-saving lie.''

''One of the many reasons it was best that I exit the political world,'' Luke said dryly. ''How well she knows me,'' he added, using his hand on her shoulder to draw Brenna even closer to him.

''But if Luke didn't make up that sperm bank story, then…then *you* were the one who did, Brenna?'' Lisa gasped at the implication. ''But why?''

''I didn't—'' Brenna began.

''She didn't want to marry me,'' Luke cut in smoothly. ''She still doesn't. Nor does she want my name on the baby's birth certificate. But I'm not giving up. Brenna is going to be Mrs. Luke Minteer, if not before the baby is born, then afterward. Count on it.''

''No,'' cried Brenna, feeling tears burn in her eyes and chiding herself for them.

This sudden urge to cry at the drop of the clichéd hat had to stop. But just hearing Luke talk about marriage, something she'd never aspired to—because she felt it was out of reach for someone with her past?—made her want to weep.

''I won't take no for an answer, honey. You know us Minteers, Ma.'' Luke flashed a grin at his mother. ''You didn't raise us to be quitters.''

''Oh, Luke, we thought—we were sure—'' Lisa was

chagrined. "I'm so sorry. I'll call Cassie right away and set the record straight."

"Why don't you want to marry my brother?" Anne Marie demanded of Brenna at the same time Rosemary was asking her, "Why don't you want to marry my son?"

Brenna felt the way she had on that long-ago night in the hospital, when the nurse had given her a shot of something "to calm her nerves."

Everything seemed unreal. Voices floated around her, but nothing being said made much sense. Faces seemed to morph wildly from one expression into the next, and it was hard to interpret them quickly enough to keep up.

The strength of Luke's arm holding her tightly against his solid, warm body was real, though. He was her anchor in this sea of confusion; his smile and his warm blue eyes were like a touchstone.

She'd had no one to cling to on that drugged night in the hospital so long ago, but today she had someone. She had Luke Minteer—who claimed he was going to marry her?

"Mom, Anne Marie, don't badger Brenna, that's my job," Luke said dryly. "Anyway, it shouldn't be any mystery why she doesn't want to marry me. Why would any woman want to marry a snake like me? I'm a cruel, big shot storyteller, I'm the family disgrace. Hardly the man of your dreams, right, Brenna?"

An uncomfortable silence descended. There was regret written all over the faces of the three Minteer women.

Brenna glanced up at Luke, who was grinning broadly, clearly on the verge of laughing out loud. Obviously, he'd heard everything his relatives had said about him and was thoroughly enjoying using their own arguments against himself.

She contemplated this glimpse into Luke's relationship with his family. They took many things very seriously, and he was a natural-born teaser who couldn't pass up a chance to needle them. They loved each other, but the chemistry was wrong.

Sometimes that happened within families, the nuns had said in an attempt to explain messed-up familial relationships to the girls back at the Denver school. Though the girls couldn't choose their relatives, they could wisely choose partners who fit with them in all the right ways. A simple message, but the words had apparently struck a chord with Brenna, because they were playing in her head right now.

She thought of her own responses to Luke. When he teased or baited her, she needled him right back. Sometimes she mocked him first. Their senses of humor were in tune. The chemistry was right.

Luke met her eyes, and their gazes locked. Brenna felt herself being drawn into his sensual blue depths and was instantly flooded with memories of making love with him. How he'd felt inside her, smooth and hot and hard, filling her up...

Oh, yes, the chemistry between them was right in ways the good sisters had *never* mentioned. And now Luke was talking about marrying her—to spare her from becoming Today's Big News on the gossip grapevine? He knew how she felt about that.

And though she loved him even more for his quixotic gesture, she couldn't take him up on it.

Brenna pulled away from him and moved quickly into the entrance foyer.

"Time to go." She opened the front door and held it open, impervious to the cold air rushing in. "'Bye, everybody. Thanks for dropping by."

Ten

"She's kicking us out," Luke explained to his mother, Anne Marie and Lisa. All of them had followed Brenna into the foyer. "You three had better go, since you don't enjoy making unwelcome pests of yourselves. Since that's never bothered me, I'm staying."

"I have to ask Brenna one question before I leave." Anne Marie planted herself directly in front of Brenna. "You're obviously in love with my brother. You flew to his defense, you said he's kind and loving and patient and understanding. Believe me, you'd have to be *madly* in love with Luke to see him that way. And you're having his baby, so why won't you marry him?"

"Maybe it's the likes of us that are keeping her from marrying Luke," Rosemary said sorrowfully. "After all, there are so many Minteers and we're too nosy, too opinionated, too close—maybe too much of everything for this quiet little girl. Our reputation has scared her off, and she doesn't want her or her baby to be Minteers. We've only ourselves to blame.''

"Oh, no, that's not true at all!" exclaimed Brenna, aghast that she'd hurt the older woman's feelings. "It's just the opposite, in fact. You wouldn't want *me* to be a Minteer!''

"And why not?" pressed Rosemary.

"You didn't approve of Luke's dirty tricks, and you hated his book," Brenna said nervously. "And if…if you think he's a disgrace, well—''

"We don't condone bad behavior, and we don't like reading about immoral criminals, that's true," his mother agreed. "But that has nothing to do with you, dear.''

"Disgrace and bad behavior and criminals have everything to do with me. My mother is in prison for murder," Brenna blurted out.

"Brenna, Brenna, Brenna." Luke pulled her away from the door with one hand and pushed it shut with the other.

She was shivering from the cold, and he wrapped his arms around her swollen belly, and held her back against him. "I can't believe you fell for Ma's sad-eyed, guilt-inducing routine. That hasn't worked on me since I was about three years old.''

"Two," his mother corrected. "And it's not a routine. I am sad that Brenna feels we would judge her, based on her mother's actions. There's certainly been a murderer or two among the Minteers.''

"There has?" Anne Marie's ears perked. "Who? When?''

"Over in Ireland, before the grandparents came to this country, and it's not up for discussion, miss," Rosemary replied so quickly that Brenna knew she was making the whole thing up to put Brenna at ease. *There's a murderer in your family? No problem, we've got them, too. Doesn't everyone?*

Brenna gave Luke's mother a tremulous smile. Unconsciously she relaxed against Luke. His body surrounded her, warming her with his male heat.

He spread his fingers wide, and they spanned nearly the entire circumference of her belly. The baby began to turn and roll and kick, as if acknowledging Luke's presence.

He kneaded gently, and Brenna almost sighed with contentment. If there hadn't been witnesses, she knew she would have sighed. But the presence of the Minteer women was effectively inhibiting.

"Brenna would like to keep the whole matter about her mother private, Anne Marie," Luke told his sister sternly. "She doesn't want it blabbed all over town. That goes for you too, Lisa. Both of you, keep your mouths shut. I know you'll convince them to keep this confidential, Ma," he urged his mother.

"Of course. We respect Brenna's privacy and won't say a word," Rosemary promised.

"He makes us sound like horrid gossips and we're not!" complained Anne Marie, shooting her brother a baleful glance. "You can trust us, Brenna. We wouldn't dream of telling anybody anything."

"Except I am going to tell Cassie Walsh that Luke wants to marry Brenna," Lisa put in. "And that he's just waiting for her to set the date. It's not fair to brand Luke as a rat who won't accept responsibility when it's not true."

"My family's staunch support of me is touching." Luke smiled sardonically. "Now, the sooner the three of you are on your way, the sooner Brenna and I can go out to eat. Baby X is starving in here." He rubbed her belly.

The trio trooped out to their car, and Brenna and Luke stood in the foyer, the door open, watching until the vehicle was out of sight.

Luke released Brenna from his hold. "I thought they'd never leave! Get your coat and we'll—"

"We can't just casually go out for dinner and act as if nothing's happened!" she exclaimed. "Your family thinks my baby is yours! They expect you to marry me!"

"And your point is?"

"Luke, we're not getting married."

"Sure we are, sweetheart. And my name is going to be on the baby's birth certificate on the line that says 'father.'"

"Luke, your family might've thought the sperm bank in Philadelphia story was far-fetched, but it's the truth," Brenna reminded him.

"It's also irrelevant, because I'm the only father the baby is going to know. I'll be a very good father, Brenna," he added seriously.

"I know you will, Luke. Someday, to your own child. But this is my child, and I can't stay here and have your family try to pressure you into marrying me and then condemn you when it doesn't happen. I—I'm moving back to Denver. I have to."

"Listen to yourself, Brenna," Luke said sharply. "Planning to run away. Dragging your child off to somewhere else because suddenly things aren't going exactly the way you wanted. Doesn't that strike you as a familiar pattern? One you promised yourself never to follow?"

"Luke, that's not fair. This situation is nothing like—"

"Here's something else to think about, Brenna. If a man wanted to stick around and try to work things out, your mother took off because she felt trapped. Is that how you feel now, Brenna? Trapped?"

Brenna swallowed hard. She felt weak and weepy and tried to work up some indignant wrath to bolster herself. "You're badgering me," she said huskily, failing to stir up either indignation and wrath.

"Of course I am." Luke laughed softly. "Didn't you hear me tell Ma and Annie that was my job?"

"You really are incorrigible." Brenna grimaced. "And you've been this way since the age of two? Your poor mother!"

"I was a hellion, all right. The family is convinced that I still am. But that's not how you see me, is it, Brenna?" Luke's voice lowered. "I was standing in the hall when I heard you defend me. I heard everything you said about me, calling me kind and loving and patient and understanding. Saying that I would never shirk responsibility for a child. You told my family they didn't know me but you did, and the person you described—"

"I described you, Luke," Brenna assured him.

"Anne Marie is right. You must be madly in love with me if you see me like that. Are you going to admit it or play it cool, Brenna?"

Brenna heaved a resigned sigh. "Oh, what's the point in trying to play it cool? I've never been cool. Yes, Luke, I love you. You know perfectly well that I do."

A wide smile crossed Luke's face, and he swiftly yanked her into his arms. "So why are you giving me such a hard time? Spouting this nonsense about going back to Denver, about not marrying me."

"Until a very short while ago, you'd never even mentioned marrying me," Brenna pointed out. "You didn't ask me to marry you, and I certainly didn't expect you to. After all, you don't love me and—"

"Oh, what's the point in trying to play it cool? Though I've always been cool, there are times when I don't need to be. I love you, Brenna," Luke paraphrased her own declaration, his blue eyes warm with humor. "And after I got that call from Saraceni, I decided to speed things along even more, so I called my cousin Patrick and told him to tell his mother that I had a pregnant girlfriend. Aunt Eileen and my mom were best friends before they were sisters-in-law, so I knew how fast that news would fly."

"Speed things along when everything has been moving at the sound of light, anyway?" Brenna smiled as tears slowly trickled down her cheeks.

"And if you didn't know it before, I want you to be sure of it now, my love," he murmured, his lips brushing her forehead. "I want to be the man I am in your eyes. I want to be the father to our baby. This one," he patted her stomach, "and whoever comes next. Say yes, Brenna. Say you'll marry me."

She was laughing and crying at the same time. "I'm an emotional basket case right now," she warned him.

"All the better to take full advantage of you, my sweet." Luke swept her up in his arms.

She clung to him, holding on tight. "You sound like the Big Bad Wolf in a fractured fairy tale."

"And didn't Big Bad and Little Red end up in somebody's bedroom?" Luke fractured the fairy tale even more.

They made it the whole way to Brenna's bedroom before Brenna told him, Yes, she would marry him.

"I wasn't going to go back to Denver," she admitted. "Not really."

"I know. You were panicking but I had to let you know how serious I am about you. I knew it wasn't the time to toss off a glib, 'Denver? Cool! I'll help you pack.'"

"You know me so well," she borrowed his words, and they both laughed.

Very quickly the laughter turned into kissing. Deep, lingering kisses accompanied by caresses that grew more intimate as they took turns removing every item of clothing from each other.

Their passion was burning hot, their actions tender and desultory, and before long they were both naked.

Together they lay back on the bed.

"I love you, Brenna," Luke murmured huskily, kissing her swollen belly. He smoothed his cheek over it, feeling the movements of the baby within. His baby. "I love both of you."

"I love you, Luke," she heard herself say, and the words evoked an emotional power that emboldened her.

His tongue explored her navel, and she combed her fingers through his hair, feeling the springy thick texture, tracing his scalp.

His lips closed over her right nipple, and he suckled gently, erotically.

Brenna gasped.

"Did I hurt you?" he asked, raising his head, instantly solicitous.

"No." She somehow remembered to breathe. "I just saw fireworks in my head again." Her body was humming, her mind floating.

"Now let's try for a Zambelli International Finale," kidded Luke, pulling her over him.

He cupped her, positioning her to receive him, and her moan of anticipation urged him to slide in farther.

He moved and she rocked back and forth, tentatively at first, then with more confidence and power, matching her rhythm to his.

His pace became hot and feral, and she kept right up with him, her head tilted back, her eyes closed in ecstasy. His hands were everywhere, on her belly and her breasts, her thighs, between them.

Brenna was overwhelmed with sensation. He was so deep. Deeper and deeper. She lost the rhythm she'd been carefully keeping and abandoned herself to the exhilaration of Luke moving within her. White-hot pleasure rocketed through her, sending her soaring.

She could feel the climax building, her body tensing.

"Let go," Luke rasped. "Let it happen. I've got you, sweetheart, you're safe with me."

And she knew she was and always would be. She let go

and went tumbling into a glittering, perfect, oblivion. Luke was with her all the way.

They sent out for pizza around ten o'clock, a late dinner but the happiest, most romantic one either had ever had.

Later Luke called his parents.

"Good news, Ma," he said exuberantly. "We're engaged. Sure, I'll tell her. But, here, why don't you tell her yourself?" He handed the receiver to Brenna.

She clutched it, a little nervously. After all, she'd pretty much kicked her future mother-in-law out of her house only hours before. "Hi, Mrs. Minteer."

"Call me Rosemary and welcome to the family, Brenna, darling. You're perfect for our Luke. It's as if you were special-ordered for him."

"Now that you mention it, I was, kind of. And he was for me, too." Brenna's eyes sparkled. "By the Cambria County Jury Commissioners."

Epilogue

It snowed on Christmas Eve, just a light coating of white on the ground to make it the traditional, nostalgic white Christmas of movie and song. Brenna and Luke saw the snowfall because they were up twice that night. Little Jack Morgan Minteer demanded milk every four to five hours around the clock.

After his 4:00 a.m. feeding, baby Jack decided not to go back to sleep and remained wakeful in his parents' bed, gazing at their faces with his big, serious dark eyes. The infant clutched his father's big finger tightly.

"Hey, little guy, Santa Claus doesn't come until the kids are sleeping, you know," Luke said softly.

Jack seemed unconcerned. There was a pile of wrapped presents under the Christmas tree, many with his name on them. Who needed Santa Claus?

"He's growing so fast." Brenna sighed with wistful, maternal pride as she stared down at her son. "Look how well he fits into this little red suit that was too big for him only two weeks ago.''

"Good thing he's got a closetful of sharp new clothes to grow into.'' Luke leaned down to smooth a lock of hair from Brenna's cheek. "He's so beautiful, Brenna. Everybody says he's the most beautiful baby they've ever seen, and they aren't just saying it to be polite—they really mean it!''

Brenna smiled. "All babies are beautiful to their family, Luke.''

"Yeah, yeah, but Jack is extra special. He looks just like you, Brenna. The dark eyes, the hair, even the shape of his little ears. They're yours. Are you sure you didn't have yourself cloned in Philadelphia?''

She chuckled and snuggled back against him. "Your mom and grandma told me Jack is the spitting image of you when you were a baby. Except your eyes were blue, of course. They plan to dig up the old photos to prove it.''

Brenna and Luke exchanged amused glances.

He kissed her gently, his arms encircling her and the baby. "Jack's mine, Bren. I couldn't love him more if I'd been there the day he was conceived.''

"I know. And you were the one to give him his name. Jack Morgan. You said I should call him after my father. I hadn't considered it till then. After I lost him, it hurt so much to think of my dad, I wouldn't let myself.''

But building her new life and a family with Luke had allowed her to access those good memories from so long ago. To honor the late Jack Morgan with a namesake.

Luke himself had filled in the baby's birth certificate.

Child's Name: Jack Morgan Minteer. Father: Luke Minteer. Mother: Brenna Morgan Minteer.

They were a family, now and forever.

*   *   *   *   *

#1 *New York Times* bestselling author

NORA ROBERTS

brings you more of the loyal and loving,
tempestuous and tantalizing Stanislaski family.

Coming in February 2001

The Stanislaski Sisters

Natasha and Rachel

Though raised in the Old World traditions of their
family, fiery Natasha Stanislaski and cool, classy
Rachel Stanislaski are ready for a *new* world of love....

*And also available in February 2001 from
Silhouette Special Edition, the newest book in the
heartwarming Stanislaski saga*

CONSIDERING KATE

Natasha and Spencer Kimball's daughter Kate turns her
back on old dreams and returns to her hometown, where
she finds the *man* of her dreams.

Available at your favorite retail outlet.

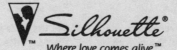
Where love comes alive™

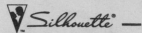

SILHOUETTE® Desire®

Get ready to enter the exclusive, masculine world of the...

TEXAS Cattleman's Club

Silhouette Desire®'s powerful new miniseries features five wealthy Texas bachelors—all members of the state's most prestigious club—who set out on a mission to rescue a princess...and find true love!

TEXAS MILLIONAIRE—August 1999
by Dixie Browning (SD #1232)
CINDERELLA'S TYCOON—September 1999
by Caroline Cross (SD #1238)
BILLIONAIRE BRIDEGROOM—October 1999
by Peggy Moreland (SD #1244)
SECRET AGENT DAD—November 1999
by Metsy Hingle (SD #1250)
LONE STAR PRINCE—December 1999
by Cindy Gerard (SD #1256)

Available at your favorite retail outlet.

Silhouette®

ATTENTION **JOAN JOHNSTON** FANS!

Silhouette Books is proud to present

HAWK'S WAY
BACHELORS

The first three novels in
the bestselling Hawk's Way series
now in one fabulous collection!

On Sale December 2000

THE RANCHER AND THE RUNAWAY BRIDE
Brawny rancher Adam Phillips has his hands full when
Tate Whitelaw's overprotective, bossy brothers show up with
shotguns in hand!

THE COWBOY AND THE PRINCESS
Ornery cowboy Faron Whitelaw is caught off-guard
when breathtakingly beautiful Belinda Prescott proves to be
more than a gold digger!

THE WRANGLER AND THE RICH GIRL
Sparks fly when Texas debutante Candy Baylor makes handsome
horse breeder Garth Whitelaw an offer he can't refuse!

**HAWK'S WAY: Where the Whitelaws of Texas
run free...till passion brands their hearts.**

"Joan Johnston does contemporary Westerns to perfection."
–Publishers Weekly

Available at your favorite retail outlet.

Coming in January 2001 from Silhouette Books...

ChildFinders, Inc.:
An Uncommon Hero

by

MARIE FERRARELLA

**the latest installment of
this bestselling author's popular miniseries.**

The assignment seemed straightforward: track down the woman who
had stolen a boy and return him to his father. But ChildFinders, Inc.
had been duped, and Ben Underwood soon discovered that nothing
about the case was as it seemed. Gina Wassel, the supposed kidnapper,
was everything Ben had dreamed of in a woman, and suddenly he had
to untangle the truth from the lies—before it was too late.

Available at your favorite retail outlet.

Where love comes alive™

Silhouette® Desire®

COMING NEXT MONTH

#1339 TALL, DARK & WESTERN—Anne Marie Winston
Man of the Month
Widowed rancher Marty Stryker needed a wife for his young daughter, so he placed an ad in the paper. When attractive young widow Juliette Duchenay answered his ad, the chemistry between them was undeniable. Marty knew he was falling for Juliette, but could he risk his heart for a second chance at love and family?

#1340 MILLIONAIRE M.D.—Jennifer Greene
Texas Cattleman's Club: Lone Star Jewels
When Winona Raye discovered a baby girl on her doorstep, wealthy surgeon Justin Webb proposed a marriage of convenience to give the child a family. But for Winona, living under the same roof with the sexy doctor proved to be a challenge. Because now that Justin had the opportunity to get close to Winona, he was determined to win her heart.

#1341 SHEIKH'S WOMAN—Alexandra Sellers
Sons of the Desert
Anna Lamb woke with no memory of her newborn baby, or of the tall, dark and handsome sheikh who claimed to be her husband. Although she was irresistibly drawn to Ishaq Ahmadi, Anna couldn't understand his anger and suspicion until the sheikh revealed his identity...and his shocking reasons for claiming *her* as his woman....

#1342 THE BARONS OF TEXAS: KIT—Fayrene Preston
The Barons of Texas
Kit Baron was in serious trouble. One of her ranch hands was dead, and she was the only suspect. Then criminal lawyer Des Baron—the stepcousin Kit had always secretly loved— came to her rescue. Now he was determined to prove her innocence, but could Kit prove her love for Des?

#1343 THE EARL'S SECRET—Kathryn Jensen
When American tour guide Jennifer Murphy met the dashing young Earl Christopher Smythe in Scotland, sparks flew. Before long their relationship became a passionate affair and Jennifer fell in love with Christopher. But the sexy earl had a secret, and in order to win the man of her dreams, Jennifer would have to uncover the truth....

#1344 A COWBOY, A BRIDE & A WEDDING VOW—Shirley Rogers
Cowboy Jake McCall never knew he was a father until Catherine St. John's son knocked on his door. In order to get to know his son, Jake convinced Catherine to stay on his ranch for the summer. Could the determined cowboy rekindle the passion between them and persuade Catherine to stay a lifetime?